GIVE A DEVIL HIS DUE

MAYA DANIELS

GIVE A
DEVIL
HIS DUE

MAYA DANIELS

vinci
BOOKS

By Maya Daniels

The Broken Halos Series

The Devil is in the Details

Speak of the Devil

Encounter with the Devil

The Devil in Disguise

To Look the Devil in the Eye

Better the Devil You Know

Give a Devil His Due

Vinci Books

vinci-books.com

Published by Vinci Books Ltd in 2025

1

The publisher and the author have made every effort to obtain permissions for any third party material used in this book and to comply with copyright law. Any queries in this respect should be brought to the attention of the publisher and any omissions will be corrected in future editions.

A CIP catalogue record for this book is available from the British Library.

Paperback ISBN: 9781036706715

The EU GPSR authorised representative is Logos Europe, 9 rue Nicolas Poussion, 17000 La Rochelle, France contact@logoseurope.eu

Chapter One

HELENA

I failed.

Miserably and absolutely failed, and not just humanity but myself and everyone I love. How's that for a wake up call? The gray sky permanently scowling in my direction and the jutting remains of the destroyed city of Atlanta reaching for it mock me without regret. Tightening the hold around my knees, I press them harder to my chest like that will lighten the crushing guilt squeezing my lungs and preventing me from taking a full breath. The only good thing that comes from it is that it stops my body from shaking at times like this when the pain is too much to bear.

"You cannot hide here forever, Helena." Raphael's voice comes as a murmur from behind me.

Not having a reaction to the sudden sound might come as a surprise to the Archangel, but I know he has been standing there hiding in the shadows for almost an hour. That's all he has done since we returned from Purgatory. Stalks me like he expects me to fall apart or lose my shit without warning.

1

"I can try." A heavy sigh trembles through my numb lips, and I twist my head to look at him over my shoulder. "Might as well join me, Raphael, and speak your peace. We both know Eric will find my hidey hole sooner rather than later. Both of you are proving to be a pain in my ass lately."

"Maybe if you talk to us, we won't worry as much about your state of mind." Rooftiles crack and shift under his boots when he gingerly moves to where I'm perched on top of the safe house. With a wary look around, he lowers his tall frame, his arm brushing mine when he plops down. "It's not just you who has all of us on edge. Your emotions affect the Trowe, as well. The last thing we need is to lose control of the spirit and him destroying whatever is left of the city."

It's been few days since we returned, and I still can't get over what I found. In the middle of the fight, things didn't look that bad around me. Stupidly, I thought we would win this war with the jinn if I sacrificed myself. Because that's what they wanted, wasn't it? To remove the abomination so things could be balanced. Instead, it turned out I, of all things, *am* the balance, and those assholes want chaos to rule so they can seize control of Heaven and Hell.

My breathing sounds too loud in the silence surrounding me and Raphael on the roof. "You don't need to worry about Narsi or me. We will do whatever is necessary to fix this mess." My hand flips around, encompassing the destroyed world before our eyes. "All of this is my fault." Pretending I don't notice the side-eyed glance he throws my way, I keep my eyes locked on the plumes of smoke cousring up from parts of Atlanta where the hunters are burning whatever bodies they can find.

Not many of the hunters are left standing, either. The ones we can spare are standing guard at the still-open portals in case additional monsters poke their cursed

2

heads out and join their brethren in the human realm in order to erase it from existence. I'd like to blame them for being dumb and guided by their evil, bloodthirsty mindsets, but it's not like I'm better than them. The fact that if the human realm falls it'll destroy Heaven and Hell has never stopped me from making idiotic, selfish decisions. Maybe it will be for the best if everything goes to shit and time resets itself. Whatever new humans, angels, and demons are created might make better choices than we ever will.

The faces of those lost float in my mind's eye, taunting me and souring the taste in my mouth. My best friend—along with the man who raised me as his own child despite what it meant for him with the Order—my other friends succumbing to the jinn, and the demons trying to make a living away from the hatred the Archangels and Archdemons fanned all flicker one face after another until my head spins, and I clutch it between my hands.

"Hel." Raphael's hand is a warm and solid weight on my shoulder, pulling me back from the madness I'm drowning in. "Thinking of what could've been or should've been will change nothing."

"You mean I shouldn't feel like the lowest piece of shit for causing the apocalypse?" Laughter bursts from me, cold and unhinged. "I should brush it off all the lives that were lost so I could sit here and watch humanity die off. You are right, we should have a party because I lived."

Tears burn the back of my eyes, but I refuse to let them fall. Everyone who died does not need me crying. No amount of tears will bring them back or give any meaning to their deaths. I should've cried before they were lost. Maybe if I did better, if I made different decisions, they could've lived even if I was no longer among them. Too many maybes and not enough tears to absolve me from my sins. Everything in me quieted with Raphael's next words.

"Let me not pray to be sheltered from dangers, but to be fearless in facing them." His fingers move a strand of my hair, tucking it behind my ear when I turn my head to face him. The sad smile on his face burns in my chest like a dagger being twisted there. "Let me not beg for the stilling of my pain, but for the heart to conquer it."

"Quoting Tagore should make me feel better for all I've done?" My snort forms a line between his brows, and for the first time, I see the turmoil brewing in his golden eyes. "We did this Raphael. Well, *I* did this, and the rest of you followed in some dumb quest to protect me and keep me alive. For what exactly? How is my life worth more than theirs?"

"My Father has a plan for all of us, Helena. Even when we don't understand it, it's best not to fight it. I'm sure things will become clear … eventually." His pep talk would be more convincing if he didn't look like he didn't believe his own words. I was happy to enlighten him on that little fact.

"Like Michael going missing? Let's not forget Lucifer." Tapping a finger on my lips, I pretend like I'm thinking about it. "Oh, right. Satanael being chained like a dog or my mother being killed played integral parts in that plan, too. I think I see the bigger picture now. You are absolutely right. There must be a superior plan in the works, and all the humans were just sacrifices in some cosmic ritual for a better future to please the Devine."

"Hel—"

"You should've left me there, Raphael." His sharp intake of breath should make me to shut up, but it doesn't.

4

"If it was me they wanted, it would've been a worthy sacrifice to save humanity."

"How dare you spit on everything we have done." Raphael unfolds to his full height until an Archangel is looming over me instead of the man I know. "We all pay penance for our actions, and all of us have lost too much to give up now. Faith is all some of us have left, and I'll be damned if I let you take that away by dwelling on memories of how things should've been." Fists clenching at his sides, he leans forward to lock gazes with me. "So stay here and romanticize about what the world would've been like if you didn't exist, but do it fast, Helena. When you are done living in the past, join us to form a plan for the future—one wearing a cloak of reality, not wishy-washy dreams."

Watching him storm off the roof, I struggle to hold my tears back. With a sigh, I turn to stare at the city, an occasional shout or screech from a dying demon reaching my ears. Raphael is right in everything he said, but I'm not sure I can move on from the memories pressing like a mountain on my chest. If the suffering I inflict on myself doesn't end, I might be a ticking bomb walking among what's left of this world, but that brings another question to mind. If I don't want to look at what's left in my wake, why am I fighting so hard to be here now? Uninvited, a memory I fight so hard to suppress blooms in my head, and it's too loud and too vivid to ignore.

"We are the Fates." Three voices boom, the power behind them dropping me on my knees. "You shall keep the balance of the realms in our name. The Archangel Raphael will be bound to your life. Lucifer's son will be bound to your heart. If you fail, you will answer to us. Your life will be ours to do as we see fit."

My shaking hand pushes the hair falling in my eyes, and I grab a fistful of it as my lids squeeze shut. The sting on my scalp grounds me from the whirlwind of pain and guilt threatening to sweep me under and let me drown. I didn't fight to survive just for myself. It was for Eric and Raphael as well. Another selfish decision on my part, but I can't find it in me to regret that one. There is nothing I wouldn't do for them. *Let's not pretend there is not something else you are trying to avoid, too.* A voice in my head sounding an awful lot like my father's reminds me of things I don't want to voice, and I suck in a breath.

Pushing off the rooftiles, I stand and face broken Atlanta with a new determination. *Your mother lives.* Those words, which I had shoved into the deepest corners of my soul, mock me. Maybe there is a way to fix all the wrongs. Zadkiel, after all, is Mercy of God, right? My mother, if – and that is a huge if to hang my hopes on – she is alive, could change things. Right? Raphael said we need faith, so I just have to believe in that.

A plan forms slowly as I crawl inside the safe house, leaving the destruction behind. Too busy to alleviate my guilt, it never dawns on me why Raphael stormed off the roof instead of flying away like he always does when he gets upset. That should've told me things were worse than I imagined.

But as always, I missed the clues the fates wave in my face.

Chapter Two

ERIC

"Have you heard back from Maddison?" My grunt turns the question into something my twin brother can make a mockery of.

"If it's too heavy, brother, go work with the rest of the humans. Leave the harder stuff for those of us with enhanced strength and speed." Colt chortles at my glare, while I'm balancing half of a building on my shoulders. "As for our dear cousin, I believe she might be busy making baby demons with Leviathan somewhere on some island. Knowing her, sex is always more important than anything else."

After the tilted wall falls into the foundation and the building rights itself, I dust off my hands and roll my shoulders. No matter how many of them we push back into place, the city stays the same. A deserted place full of dust and smoke. I don't miss the tears Helena tries to hide, nor the pain she pretends not to feel. My mate's nightmares are getting worse, and I need Maddison to help me understand how to help the female I love.

"Don't be a prick, Colt, she will never walk away from a fight. Especially not one that can get all of us killed." Hands on my hips, I turn to search for something else I can fix before the hunters shepherd the humans in need of a shelter this way. "For all we know, they might be imprisoned along with your father."

"Lucifer is your father, too, dear brother." My fingers twitch on my hip with the urge to punch the grin off his face. "But you can go looking for them if it is your wish. I'll make sure your mate is warm and taken care off. What are brothers for if not to help each other out?"

Beating me to is, Beelzebub's meaty fist connects to the side of Colt's head, throwing it back and spinning his body around. My father's confidant proceeds to beat my brother in a whirl of fists and kicks until both of them are a bloody mess sprawled on the dirt and panting for breath.

"Fuck, I needed that." Beelzebub grunts, rolling back on his feet.

"Me, too." Colt joins him, dabbing the back of his hand over his split lip. "I need something to kill, not to crawl over broken buildings and bridges. Don't humans have machines that do these things?"

"George gave the hunters orders to call us when they come across demons or anything not of this world." I ignore his comment about machines. The last thing we need is to make noise some creature will want to investigate when we have no idea what has crawled out in this realm. Yet, I still look at the walkie-talkie hanging from my belt and poke at it like that will make it say something. "Raphael is supervising them, too. I'm sure they'll call for us soon."

"Leave it to the Archangel to lord over everything instead of getting his hands dirty with the rest of us common folk." Colt spits a glob of blood on the ground, his mouth twisting in disgust. "Call the Haltija to do this shit, I'm done. I'll go hunt myself. You coming?" He aims his question to Beelzebub.

Whatever the answer is going to be gets lost in the whoosh of wind that blasts debris and plaster in the air to pelt our skin. Not long behind it, a form casts a shadow over the three of us, blotting whatever weak light the sun is pushing through the clouds of smoke from above Atlanta. It looks like my brother's wishes are manifesting when two more demons join the first one, all of them coming at us fast from the sky.

"All you have to do is ask and ye shall receive," I mutter under my breath as I brace myself for the attack.

"Hell's balls," Colt snorts. "He is starting to sound like Raphael, too. Soon he will sprout white feathers and grow a halo instead of horns."

The demons are of the high classes in Hell, and they hit hard, cutting off any retort I have for my idiot twin. After returning from Purgatory, I learned that any of them left in the human realm were not much for talking or spewing threats at us, unlike when Abaddon was in charge. They attack hard and fight with the desperation of males who need to prove something. Be it their worth or to justify their stupidity for following a loose cannon, I'm not sure, nor do I care. It gives us an outlet to aim our rage at, and that's all that matters.

We fall into a familiar dance of twists and turns, the three of us back-to-back and the demons come at us from all directions, looking for an opening. A coppery scent and the stench of sulfur saturates the air and clogs my nose with each breath I take. Soon it becomes clear we don't want to fight to end it too soon, all of us allowing the feral demons to score hits and shred our skin. Pained grunts and roars echo across the empty street, bouncing off the walls of the buildings we managed to salvage. I'm sure we can drag this out until we tire and then kill the fuckers, but just as I'm thinking that a shrill scream comes from nearby, and it costs me the use of my right arm.

Claws sink into my shoulder, gauging the flesh and shredding my skin. A ferocious roar rips from my chest when the bone is yanked out of its socket, and I lash out wildly at the idiot attacking me. My fist connects to the center of his chest, and his body sails through the air before it hits the wall of the closest building, breaking a hole through it twice as large as he is. So much for salvaging whatever is left of the city.

"Kill them. The humans need our help." Snarling, I grind my teeth and jerk my arm back. The crack of the joint sliding into place sets my teeth on edge and fuels my anger. "Stop playing games before more lives are lost."

"I'm telling you," Colt sneers, ducking to avoid a punch to his face and pummels the demon into a bloody pulp before huffing in annoyance. "Every day he sound more like the Archangel than a Prince of Hell. It's disgusting."

"Your face is disgusting as well, yet I have to look at it daily." Beelzebub sighs, shaking blood and gore from his fingers. "Lead the way, Shadow. The sooner we get to the threat, the less the chances are you'll be Lucifer's only child."

"You are aware that we look alike." Beelzebub grins at my comment when he falls into step with me. "But my guess is, that was your point."

With a shrug, he takes to the sky, and we do too. It's difficult to reach the humans unless you have wings. The streets are either cracked open with craters deep enough to kill whoever falls in them, or they are blocked from crumbled structures that didn't survive the attack the jinn orchestrated. Colt's grumbling follows behind us like an annoying insect refusing to remove itself from the shell of our ears.

"I'm worried about Helena." Not sure what I expect from Beelzebub, but the troubled look crossing his face is not it.

"Let us deal with the scum first."

He and Colt round the corner, leaving me behind to drown in my thoughts. Whatever is down there with the humans is not really a threat to one, little less three of us. The two of them will deal with it much better than I can deal with my own internal demons—the ones inside me that are doing their damn best to drive me insane. My mate needs help, and I'm helpless to aid her.

"Maybe we can all talk to her." I blink Beelzebub into focus, and a frown scrunches my face. How long was I hovering in the air lost in my head? "It was just a handful of rogues. All sorted now." He offers an explanation, misreading my confusion.

"Right." With one last look around, I scrub a hand over my face just as Colt joins us. "We should go back and ..." Glancing between the two of them, I gnaw on my lower lip. "You two can start with the questions. I'll back you up."

"You're too scared to ask your mate if she's losing her shit?" Colt looks too pleased with himself, and I wonder if I can get away with giving him a black eye. Maybe not the best idea before cornering Helena and forcing her to talk, but making him bleed will please me to no end.

"Have you met my mate?" Both of them chuckle and shake their heads like that will embarrass me. "I'm surprised your balls don't shrivel just thinking about making her talk, Colt."

"I have no intention to die this day." My brother adjusts

himself, wincing at the memory. "This was Beelzebub's idea. I'm just a back-up. A back-up who is out of there if there is a dagger in her hand. Don't say I didn't warn you."

"Both of you are pathetic." Beelzebub's bravado would work if he didn't swallow thickly when the safe house comes into view, and Helena disappears inside it from the roof. "I should know not to ask boys to do a man's job."

My feet hit the street as we drop near the front yard, and I roll my shoulders in hopes of removing the tension bunching every muscle on my body. One way or another, I must do this for my mate. She may not appreciate it at the moment, but I know Helena. She will open up if we press her hard enough, and then we will know what is haunting her dreams. Maybe I can't fight an enemy I cannot physically touch, but I sure as hell am willing to give it a try.

I'm still going to keep my mouth shut.

Beelzebub can start the questioning, even if it ends in his funeral.

I love my mate, but I definitely don't have a death wish.

Chapter Three

HELENA

Well, apart from being a failure, apparently I am a coward as well. Something that becomes abundantly clear the moment I sense Eric getting close to the safe house as I come down from my perch on the roof. I hightail it to the first empty room to hide. Lucky for me, Raphael has taught me how to retract my wings inside my body when I'm not using them, so it's easy to slip away unnoticed. Using my wings is a bit of a stretch, though, since I flop around like a half-dead pigeon a couple of feet above ground before I manage to lift in the air and every landing is with me ending up on my ass, but yeah. What I'm saying is I don't bounce off walls and doors like a pinball machine while I'm walking. The tail is a whole different matter because there is no escaping it. Now I have it wrapped around my waist so I can wear pants, which I ripped at the seam, so the only thing holding them up is my belt. It's a mess I have to live with.

I'm a mess.

"I can eat his face."

13

My heart lurches, hitting the roof of my mouth when Narsi hisses from next to me. I forgot how silently my side-kick can move when he is not resembling a tall hill of a monster. Stupidly, I thought I snuck away from him, too.

"You can't eat Eric's face, Narsi." Pressing the bridge of my nose does not help the headache throbbing at the back of my skull. "I kinda like it where it is."

"Shadow makes you uneasy. I do not like my Mistress in distress." My eyebrows climb up when he starts petting my leg lovingly. "I can eat half his face?" Those eyeless sockets lift to lock on my gaze. "Humans call it compromise."

"Now you decide to adopt some human mannerisms?" Keeping my tone low, I mutter under my breath while keeping an eye on the front entrance of the safe house through a crack in the door, which is clutched in my white-knuckled grip. "This is not up for debate. How about not eating anyone for a while. Let's start with that."

Eric, his brother, and Beelzebub march inside the house with purpose, and that's enough proof for me to justify my idea of hiding. They are up to something, and I'll bet my horns and tail it has something to do with me. My suspicions are confirmed when the twins shoulder their way behind Beelzebub and shove him forward to lead the way. Oh, yeah. Eric is definitely planning to corner me if his arrogant, grumpy ass is willing to walk behind the others. Any other time, nothing will prevent him from finding me.

"Hel," Beelzebub bellows from the top of his lungs, his boots thumping rhythmically over the hardwood floors. "I brought your mate back unharmed. He might've cried a couple of times, but nothing we can't fix. Where are you?"

Lips pressed in a firm line, I stay quiet and watch them search for me, the doors opening and closing with more force the longer they come out empty-handed. Meanwhile,

Narsi snickers gleefully next to me, his tiny body vibrating from excitement because they are getting angry. It'll be a clusterfuck in less then five minutes, but I stubbornly refuse to face them. I'm doing great ignoring everything, thank you very much, and I'd like to keep it that way.

I know the jig is up when they get Raphael to join them.

Steeling my spine, I take a deep breath and yank the door open. "Oh great, you're all back." Stepping out in the hallway, I start backing toward the entrance when all four of them poke their heads out from different rooms. "I'll go find George and Cass, and we can meet up in the common area in like an hour. Hold the forte while I'm gone." I add two thumbs up for good measure.

Spinning on my heel, I bolt for the door, but Narsi is still clinging to my damn leg, so I almost faceplant before I reach it. My shriek is cut short when a familiar calloused hands wrap around my upper arms and pulls me to a firm, unyielding chest. When Eric's scent fills my nose and my head spins from the instant need I have for him, I know my escape is not meant to be. While my brain screams for me to run and not allow them to drag me into a conversation better left alone, my body has a different plan. It turns pliant in my mate's arms, molding to him like it's meant to be in his embrace. Which I suppose is the truth of it.

"Eric, there you are." Turning inside the circle of his arms, I plant a kiss on his soft lips, and his hold loosens around me. "You rest, lover, and I'll be right back." Ducking out of his embrace while he struggles to hold back his reaction, I take one step before he yanks me back.

"And where do you think you are going, Hel?" His deep voice raises goosebumps over my arms. "The hunters are on their way. We saw them from the sky when we were returning here."

"Right." I stop struggling and offer him a strained smile. "I'll just meet them outside the wards then, just to make sure nothing is following behind them."

The house spins around, and I'm thrown over a shoulder before I'm done talking. Narsi the traitor snickers when I lift my head to glare at him through the curtain of my hair, doing some deranged happy dance with his arms flopping as he jumps in a circle. One second he wants to eat Eric's face, and the next he is okay with my mate manhandling me to wherever he feels I should be going. To add insult to injury, Eric's hand connects with my ass with a loud smack, the sting of the slap rendering me mute for a second. It speaks volumes of my mental state that I don't rip him a new one until he deposits me on my feet in the space we use for meetings.

The room is empty of everything but a long, wooden table they drug from what was left of Sanctuary and the mismatched chairs sprinkled around it. Maps marked with red and yellow lines connecting the closed and opened portals around Atlanta and her neighboring areas are spread all over it. Refusing to look at any of them, I fist my hands and stare at the spiderwebbed cracks in the empty walls above their heads. It's easy to do because all four are blocking the door in case I try to escape again.

"Okay, fine. Let's hear it." When the silence stretches to the point of driving me nuts, I fold my arms across my chest. My damn tail twitches around my waist, and my butt cheeks clench from its movement. "Out with it."

"Shadow is worried about you." Beelzebub grins like a fiend, his red eyes glittering with amusement when Eric snarls at him. "You decided I'll be the one to talk to her. I never said I won't throw you under the bus for it." One meaty shoulder rolls in the semblance of a shrug before he turns his focus back to me. "Now that I have made sure he is the one who will pay for this, I have to say we all are worried. Much as I hate to admit it, I worry about you too." Squeezing the words through clenched teeth, I watch in fascination as a muscle jumps in his square jaw.

Raphael mentioned a few times that Beelzebub is not too pleased with his concern of my wellbeing, but until now, I thought he was just trying to add to my guilt for refusing to talk with them. Locked in the Archdemon's red gaze, all my attempts to calm the galloping of my heart are futile, which doesn't go unnoticed by any of them. But what can I tell them that they don't already know? Apart from why Eric and Raphael are both standing in this room, they know most of what eats me alive.

"I have no idea what you guys want me to say." Throwing my arms up in defeat, I stomp to the table and plop my ass on the edge. Narsi inches closer and reaches for my leg, but my glare stops him from touching me. The little shit needs to learn not to switch sides when it suits him. "We failed. No matter how you look at it, because of me, the human realm paid the price. Just look around you. Was I worth all the lives lost?"

"Yes," all four answer in a choir and stare at me unblinking.

It becomes obvious I'm going to carry this weight alone because they don't understand the gravity of our actions. For them, including Raphael, a human life is but a blink of an eye and not something to mourn. If I'm being honest with myself, I haven't come to terms with my immortality yet, but I do remember all too well how aware I was of my mortal body and soul before my life turned upside down. Not long ago, I was one of the humans, regardless if that was true or not. I grew up believing I was one of those standing between them and all evil. Just because my concept of what is evil has changed doesn't mean my sense of responsibility has. Heaven, Hell, Purgatory ... they can all gouge their eyes out for all I care as long as they leave the human realm alone.

They didn't.

"I'm sorry I can't agree with you on that." Rubbing my forehead, I blow out a deep breath through pursed lips. "I can't see what's left out there"—My hand shoots out, pointing in a random direction—"and think, you know what? I'm just happy that I'm alive. To hell with all the innocents who died in the process. At first it was Abaddon, then it was the jinn, but we all must face the truth now. It was us. We did this." Swallowing the lump that formed in my throat, I don't hide my anguish from them anymore. "I did this."

"Hel." Raphael doesn't need to say anything else for me to know he is as tortured by everything that happened as I am. It's clear as day in the tone of his voice.

"No." Eric, on the other hand, has a different opinion, as always. Of course he does when it comes to me. "I will not apologize for what any of us have done. This is all on the jinn and their twisted ideas of how the realms should be. Their hunger for power is what brought us to this. A lot of lives were lost, but look at how many we have saved." With each word, he moves closer until he looms over me, and I have to crane my neck to keep eye contact. "If you want someone else to blame, then blame it on me, Hel. Because I'll tell you this once again and for the last time. I'll do it all over again and kill them all to have you here with me. I will not apologize for that. Not ever."

"As much as I love disagreeing with Eric, I have to say he makes a valid point." Raphael braves coming shoulder to shoulder with my mate. "I did the unspeakable for you, and as much as it left a mark on my very existence, I do not regret it. I can't."

"We will have to agree to disagree then." Squirming under their scrutiny, I kick Narsi away when he latches onto my leg. "No hugging now that you are not bothered by them lecturing me."

"I like my Mistress alive." My sidekick pouts, but he doesn't look apologetic at all. "You said I cannot eat Shadow's face."

The incredulous expression on Eric's face is worth all the discomfort I suffered from the conversation.

"As much as I'd love to see the Haltija munch on my brother, I would have to agree with them, she-devil. You are a pain in my ass, but the realms need you." I watch Colt saunter to the closest chair and sprawl on it, spreading his legs wide and throwing an arm over the back of it. "The human realm will recover as it always does. The damn things procreate like rabbits if you ask me. If we did nothing, it could've been much worse."

"Instead of dwelling on what could've been, maybe we should look into where Lucifer is." Beelzebub takes a page from Colt's book and grabs a chair for himself too, straddling it. "With him still missing and Leviathan who knows where, I doubt Satanael can create any sort of order in Hell. We have Michael missing as well, don't we? That makes Hell and Heaven ready to go boom at any moment. If that happens, all we did will be for nothing."

I never thought of it that way, but now anxiety churns in my stomach. For whatever reason, I dumbly believed everything was over and we just had to help rebuild the human realm. How stupid of me to think the Fates will make it as easy as all that. They let me keep Eric and Raphael, but my fight is not over. The question is, how do I go about it? Like it or not, I have to admit them forcing me to face my short-comings might just save me from carrying even more guilt on my shoulders.

"Your mother lives."

With a thick swallow, I nod at Beelzebub. "You are right. We should look for them."

"Great." Colt jumps to his feet. "I know just where to start."

The Fates help us when we need Eric's twin to lead the way.

Chapter Four

RAPHAEL

"Are you sure you are up for this?"

I crack my neck, loosening my arms at my sides. Ignoring Beelzebub and his pestering, my lungs fill with air full of smoke and the stench of death. After they planted the idea of finding the others in Helena's head, it didn't take long for everyone to agree we must begin the search. Colt's plan to enlist Satanael's help didn't sit well with me, but I was outvoted, which brought us here. In the middle of a field outside of Atlanta, where I will open a portal to Hell since we do not know how Helena's powers are changed.

Easy task for an Archangel in the human realm.

As sweat trickles down my spine and my shoulder blades itch from the need to spread my wings, I can't help but wonder what it all means for me. No matter how much I strain or push all my power into it, not even the spark of a portal appears before me.

I can't open the cursed thing.

To anywhere, not just Hell.

Keeping it to myself, I try to breach a gateway to a different city with no luck.

"Let him focus." When Eric jumps to my defense, it becomes clear I'm in real trouble.

"I can't do it." Head hanging low between my shoulders, I squeeze my eyes shut. "I can't take us anywhere."

"What do you mean 'you can't?'" Beelzebub spins me to face him with a firm grip on my arm. "The stench of Heaven is all over you, brother. Of course you can open portals. Did you hit your head on something?"

"Leave him alone, Beelzebub." Eric shoves the Archdemon away and takes his place next to me. "Purgatory, as well as the fight, took a lot from all of us. You are not recovered yet, angel."

"I'm not sure that's the problem." My muttering only makes his scowl deepen.

"It is the only problem, you dumb fuck. I feel weird too, but it'll pass." His snarl makes me swallow all the reasons why I can't do what comes natural to an Archangel.

"You are right." Avoiding Helena's searching gaze, my chin tilts up with confidence I do not feel. "My powers are sluggish after expending them so much, especially in Purgatory."

"So, what now? We are just going to stand around like idiots until you recover?" Colt huffs, kicking a rock in annoyance. "This just means you need to try harder, Archangel. Not take a break."

"You truly are your father's son, Colt." Despite everything, my mouth curls at the corners. "I thought Eric might take on his personality, but I can see Lucifer in you much better."

"If you meant it as an insult, you failed." Eric chuckles slapping my shoulder. "You just made his century." To my surprise, Colt doesn't jab at his brother, and he offers me a clipped nod.

"Maybe I can do it."

We all turn to Helena when she speaks, and she rasps her teeth over her lower lip. I can tell she is anxious by the way her fists clench and open at her sides as she shifts from foot to foot. She must be debating the wisdom of her offer because she nods to herself and squares her shoulders.

"I can do it." This time her confidence is firm.

"It's not a matter of if you can do it or not, Helena." Beelzebub latches onto the problem of testing her right now like a dog to a fresh bone. "He should do it without a second thought. What is the problem here, Raphael?"

"Why does it matter who opens a portal?" Helena hurries to defend me and squares off with the Archdemon. "We just need one to go talk to my father. I got this, plus it's a good way to practice since I have a feeling we might need it."

"That might be true because the Archangel is useless." Beelzebub sneers at me with disappointment. "Are we certain the jinn didn't replace him?"

"Not funny." Helena frowns at him when I stay silent. "I know it's Raphael and not a jinn impersonating him."

This is my punishment.

No matter how prepared I am for it, seeing it first hand when my powers and abilities fail leaves a bitter taste on my tongue. I don't regret breaking all the rules and entering Purgatory for Helena, but I'll be lying to myself if I say it's not numbing. My head swims with the gravity of my situation, and I realize my body does too when Eric grips my upper arm hard to keep me standing. Cold sweat washes over me until a small hand is pressed on my chest, and I look down at Helena's upturned face.

"It's okay, Raphael. I promise I'll fix this." Unshed tears swim in her green eyes. "I have no idea how, but I'll fix it if it's the last thing I do."

"First we need to talk to Satanael, then I can call on Gabriel." My hand covers her tiny one and I take comfort from the contact. "Gabriel is a healer, and I'm sure he can figure it out."

"We can also use his help since we have no idea what we are dealing with apart from jinn. I doubt they'll have my father and Michael ready for the taking when we do find them." Eric doesn't release the hold he has on me, and his fingers give my arm a reassuring squeeze.

I have to believe in what they are saying. Anything else means not just that I'm useless in this fight we have coming but also that I'm a liability to those I want to protect. Fortifying my will, I give them a tentative smile and step away so Helena can take my place. My heart hurts when she pulls out the dagger, her knuckles whitening where she grips it tightly. When the first drops of blood hit the dusty ground, a lurch in my chest makes me dizzy. Eric is next to her, ready to rip apart any threat coming for his mate, yet her head turns, and she looks at me.

"I have no idea what I need to do, Raphael. Apart from bleeding, how do I call on a portal to Hell?" The small curl of her lips is forced for my sake.

"Just think of your father." In two steps, I'm next to her as well, the glares from Beelzebub and Colt stabbing between my shoulder blades. "I'll guide your power." My fingers wrap around her bleeding palm, and I almost double over when her energy slams inside me in a tidal wave.

"Archangel." Eric's booming voice pulls me back before I drop on my knees.

"It was just unexpected, I'm fine." But I don't push him

24

away when he offers assistance to keep me standing, no matter how much it hurts my ego. "It won't be long now, so be ready to cross over because I cannot be sure how long we can keep it open."

"Just open it, Raphael. We will be through it before you know what's happening." Beelzebub yanks Colt closer to where we are gathered in a cluster. "Ready when you are."

With a deep breath, I guide Helena's power, and the portal blooms before my eyes faster than any opened in the history of all the realms. The colors swirling in it are unlike anything I've ever seen, but I have no time to admire them. Beelzebub darts through it first without a second thought, followed by Colt. My body keeps trembling when Eric pushes me through next, and he follows with Helena by his side.

I should've checked where it'd spit us out before I allowed everyone to cross it.

I should've, but I didn't.

Chapter Five

HELENA

"Where the fuck are we?"

I have no idea what I thought I was going to see, so it takes me back a step when some sort of a settlement appears before us. It's like we jumped back in time with the mud-packed huts and straw-covered roofs of the homes behind the tall wooden fence a few yards away from where we are standing. The dread twisting my insides worsens when Eric fidgets next to me with a frown pulling on his forehead.

"I have no clue," my mate answers my dumb question.

"Well, I was thinking of Satanael so we better go check if he is here." My feet move before I have time to start doubting everything and run away screaming. If having angel wings and demon horns and tail are supposed to make me braver, I don't notice. "Maybe he started a new hobby like farming."

Ignoring the snickering from the guys behind me, I push away the tall grass reaching my hips. On the bright side, the air doesn't smell of death, although the lack of any type of sound apart from our breathing is unsettling. Good thing we left Narsi at the safe house because I'm sure my crazy side-kick would've been stomping around this place full beast-mode in no time. The energy surrounding the settlement is pushing at all my defenses like it's telling me to turn around and get away from it.

"Judging by the wards on this place, I think we found Satanael," Colt grumbles in frustration. "Someone really needs to tell that fuck to tone it down a bit, aye?"

"What? You're Canadian now?" My focus is glued to the wide open gates of the fence, although I can't help but poke at Eric's twin. My mate and Raphael flank me on each sid,e so I'm calmer than I should be.

"I hate fucking wards." This time, the twin grunts because Beelzebub punches his shoulder.

"There is no one here." Stating the obvious is becoming my specialty. "Why is there no one here?"

A single dirt road stretches ahead of us, boarded on each side with the low huts who gape ominously and silently like sentinels guarding an empty tomb. Instead of doors, gray fabric drapes the entrances, reminding me of the gray sack I wore in Purgatory while I had to face dozens of crea-tures wearing my face and suffer the torment of being shoved through the same memory over and over again. I fist my hands hard enough for my nails to break skin just to keep myself from running, so I shift my focus to my feet where my boots are puffing out small clouds of dust with each step.

"Satanael." At Beelzebub's shout, I nearly jump out of my skin. "Show your ugly mug. We don't have time to check every hut for your ass."

"Can you stop screaming?" I hiss at him through clenched teeth. "We don't know what's waiting for us here."

"It's Hell, she-devil." Colt shoulders his way ahead of all of us, stomping like a bull on the packed dirt. "Whatever is here will answer to us."

"Right, like that worked well for you when Lucifer's home was attacked." My molars crack while I glare at his back. "Especially when they nearly killed all of us. Remember that little nugget of wisdom?"

"My daughter speaks the truth." We are almost to the middle of the settlement when Satanael's voice comes from between two huts. "You never know what waits for you around each corner."

The air is stuck in my lungs when he steps out, and a genuine smile pulls his lips wide. My hands tremble as I dart my gaze from the horns on his head to his wide chest and down to the triangular tip of his tail, which is twitching near his feet. My own tail and horns are the same color as my father's, and it takes everything in me not to walk up to him so I can touch his. The pure happiness he clearly displays keeps me frozen in place because it's unnerving.

"We need your help," I blurt out.

"We defeated the jinn." The smile slips from his face, and his features scrunch with anger. "The scum are back?"

"Can we speak somewhere that is not open for everyone to hear?" Eric's hand warms my lower back when he presses his palm there. As is the norm these days, my body leans into his touch without a conscious thought on my part.

"There is no one but us here." Just to make sure I'm not talking out of my ass, I glance to Raphael for confirmation. "Not even insects if you didn't notice."

"This way." Like I haven't said a word, Satanael turns on his heel and disappears between the two crudely made huts.

We all rush after him so we don't lose sight of his

hulking form single file to be able to fit between the structures. Beelzebub takes the front, with Raphael and Eric placing me in the middle, and Colt saunters last. Alert and wary, we follow my father through the narrow man-made path at the back of the huts until he opens a trapdoor near the end of it. With one look around to make sure no one is lurking nearby, he drops inside, leaving us to choose for ourselves how much we trust him.

It proves some have faith in Satan more than others because Beelzebub is gone next, and Raphael, out of everyone here who should doubt the decision, jumps in the hole with no pause in his step. Eric's hand is comforting when he stops me, peering down at me before offering me a nod to tell me it's safe. With a deep breath, I close my eyes and make the jump.

One second is all I have to move aside before Eric is beside me, his head swiveling so he can assess our surroundings. Colt is less graceful, especially when, judging by the smirk on his face he not so accidentally bumps into me.

"Have a seat." Satanael waves his arm with flourish like we are some mid-century upper-class gathering for a tea party.

I look up at the trapdoor when Eric pulls the rope to close it, cutting off whatever natural light coming from it. It takes a moment to adjust to the candlelight bathing everything in a warm yellow glow, and I blink at the large space. There are candles everywhere, from the floor to the walls. Velvet sofas and loveseats are placed in a circle around a fireplace large enough to fit the twins inside it without them having to bend their heads. Shelves are dug into the dirt walls, each lined with leather-bound books and bottles of booze. Some of the alcohol is on the low wooden table, and I watch like an idiot as Satanael places glasses on it as if this is a social call and he is not the Devil everyone fears.

"Bachelor pad?" Shuffling closer, I can't stop staring. It's actually quite nice for a hole in the ground.

"Even I need to escape sometimes." My father's lips twitch at the corners, no doubt because of my dumb-founded expression. "Let me hear of this help you need, Helena."

"My mother is alive."

I didn't mean to say it. I wasn't even thinking it, for fuck's sake.

You could hear a pin drop after my idiotic statement.

Chapter Six

HELENA

I startle when all five of them start yelling at once. The noise is so sudden that my feet lift about a foot off the floor, and my heart gives a solid attempt to punch out of my ribcage. One thing I have going for me is the fact that they are arguing among each other, while I'm left alone to numbly see the situation unfold like a car crash nobody can look away from.

My reprieve doesn't last long.

"It's another trick from the jinn, this time so they can trap Helena." Satanael's upper lip is curled over his teeth in a snarl. I didn't know his skin could get redder than it already is. "They used it once on me, so it will not work again. It's a ploy to imprison my daughter so I can willingly place the collar around my own neck to do their bidding."

"Zadkiel has not been seen for over twenty years. It can't be ... she cannot be alive after all that time." Raphael is on his feet, pacing back and forth like a caged lion. My skin prickles from the power he is blasting us with, and if I have to guess, I'll say he is not aware of what he is doing.

"For someone that was useless to open a portal, you sure pack a punch," Colt, never one to mince words, drawls at the display of power from the Archangel. "I don't know why we are wasting time on this nonsense. We all know it's bullshit."

All my energy goes into breathing in and out, their anger fueling my anxiety to the point I might just have a panic attack. My attention is pulled away from hyperventilating to where I'm gripping the dagger when Eric's fingers curl around mine. Shocked, I watch him lower my weapon the same way he might treat a snake ready to strike. When did I go for the dagger? And why in all the world would I do it among friends?

"Take it easy, Hel," Eric murmurs in my ear, molding his body to mine until I feel surrounded by him. "As much as I would love to kill them, sometimes we do need their help."

"I don't want to kill them." The words rush through my lips, and I drop the dagger like it's hot coal. "What the hell?"

"Step away from my daughter, Shadow." My father goes right for Eric, his snarl still in place. "Unhand her now."

"Stop," I snap at him, and he freezes in his dash to hurt my mate. "Unhand her? Really?"

"It is a human expression, is it not?" Satanael's arms cross over his chest, and he glares down his nose at Eric. "My daughter has lived among humans all this time, and I do not wish to scare her. I will tear you limb from limb for handling her like she is cattle."

My groan sounds pained to my own ears, but he keeps going.

"That is what I need here so she can visit more often instead of entertaining ludicrous ideas the jinn plant for her." Like he sees his space for the first time, he looks around while a line forms between his brows. "I need to bring humans to do everything she needs." His eyes turn on my face. "Do you wish them to be male or female? Young or old? It matters not because it shall be done." His hand slices the air with finality, and he gives me a reassuring nod like he is expecting me to shop for humans like I used to shop for shoes.

"This should be interesting," Beelzebub mumbles from his spot on the sofa he is yet to vacate.

"Stop growling." I nudge Eric when the motor in his chest kicks up. "And let's get this one thing straight before we move on to important things." My finger stabs the air in front of Satanael's nose. "We are not stealing humans so we can bring them to Hell. Are we clear?"

"Why ever not?" My father seems taken aback, while the other four wisely shake their heads and look at anything but me. "They will be honored to serve me, and you too."

"Because it's Hell." Spelling it out slowly for him doesn't help.

"I do not understand, Helena." He honestly looks puzzled by the concept that no human ever wants to see Hell.

Mind spinning on how to say what I need to say so he can grasp it, I almost give up when the idea hits me. "You haven't seen what the battle with the jinn did to Earth. There is not enough humans left for you to take even one, little less more of them." And because he doesn't seem convinced, I hurry to reassure him I'm right. "You just can't, okay? It'll upset me very much if you touch whoever is left there. I need them to stay where they are."

"They help you by simply being there?" One of his eyebrows cocks as if calling me a liar.

"Just don't touch the humans." My angry hiss makes him nod reluctantly. I have a feeling this insane conversation is not over. "Now, back to what I accidently said. It wasn't the jinn who spilled the beans that my mother was alive." With a sigh, I rub the back of my neck. "I think that's what they said at least."

I expect Raphael to jump on it, and he doesn't disappoint. From one breath to the next, he is in front of me, taking both my hands in his. Eric and Satanael stiffen, but no one says a word. My glare might have something to do with it, though.

"*They* who, Hel?" The Archangel's tone is filled with so much hope it nearly chokes me, and I can't speak for a moment. "Who told you that Zdakiel is alive?"

"The Fates."

It takes two tries to swallow the lump in my throat, and I reluctantly lift my gaze from our hands to his face. If there was any doubt how much Raphael cared about my mother, it's erased the second our gazes lock. It's like I'm looking at myself in the mirror when Eric was hurt and wouldn't wake up when we escaped from Hell. The torment is plain and clear in the swirl of his irises. That wretched feeling when you are too scared to hope but terrified to accept the horrible truth that you have to give up on someone you love.

"Raphael." Chewing on the inside of my mouth, I pick my next words carefully. Eric steps at my back, lending me his strength, and I'm grateful the rest stay silent. "It was a situation that ended with me having wings, horns, and a tail. A clusterfuck of epic proportions, if you will. I was close to death and dizzy from blood loss when everything went down. A lot of things were said as well as promised." His fingers tighten painfully on mine. "And I mean *a lot* was said. It's obviously enough for me to go searching, and I have every intention of turning all the realms inside out to see if it's true. But, I also want you to keep in mind that I could've heard wrong. In all the mess, I could've heard what I wanted to hear and not what they said."

"I understand." My heart cracks open at the sad tilt of his lips. "I will help you search no matter how long it takes."

"As will I." Satanael shoves the Archangel away, making him stumble to the side as he takes his place. "As long as it shall take, Helena." My father is oblivious to the incredulous look that's no doubt plastered all over my face.

"You don't even love my mother." My tone calls him an idiot without me saying the words.

"Love is nonsense meant for humans." Dismissing me, he shrugs unapologetically for his behavior. Zadkiel is a strong warrior and needed for holding the jinn back and away from our realms. Besides, she is your mother, and that alone is enough for my aid in your quest."

"How compassionate of you." He also misses the dryness in my voice.

"I do wish to please you."

"Thanks … I think?" Turning away from him so I don't punch the pleased look off his smug face, I dart my eyes over the others. "Well?"

"The plan was to find Lucifer, Michael, and whoever else is imprisoned by the jinn," Beelzebub muses, and Colt nods in agreement. "If Zadkiel is indeed alive, we will find her."

"Now that you mentioned it, I do need Lucifer's aid myself." My father moves around the room, shoving things in a leather satchel I didn't see him pull from anywhere. "This was a good plan, daughter."

"I aim to please, too." My eyes roll at his attitude, but as long as he tags along and brings more muscle in case it comes to a fight, he can make everything about him for all I care.

Eric stays mostly silent, but he can't hide the grin fighting to appear on his handsome face. Wrapping my arms around his waist, I press my ear on his chest, and the rhythmic beat of his heart calms my frayed nerves. Intentional or not, I'm glad I blurted out what weighed on my mind. Because at the end of the day, it's best to be prepared for whatever comes our way when we go looking. I have never been one for surprises, and I have no intention of starting now.

Maybe my wish to find my mother will finally come true.

It also occurs to me that sometimes I should be careful what I wish for.

Especially since in rare cases, I may just get it.

Chapter Seven

RAPHAEL

All of us should've expected something to go wrong, but we did not. Not once has anything gone right when Helena is involved, but I truly had faith that horrible times were behind us. The row of demons facing us when we exit the crudely made settlement says otherwise. Their eyes are on me, ignoring everyone else.

I suppose I do stand out in the middle of Hell.

"What is the meaning of this?" Satanael steps forward before I have a chance to say anything.

"Some things do not belong in Hell, my lord." A burley demon steps up, his pointed chin tilting up. "You have been gone many years and missed the changes. Give us the angel and the girl, and the rest of you can pass."

"You dare ask for my daughter?" Satanael roars in fury, his wrath pulsing around us. The tip of his tail is twitching from it.

"The girl has angel blood." The hellspawn sniffs the air. "She is no demon."

Confused, I check on Helena. Not once since I've

known her has she stayed silent. Granted, the twins and Beelzebub are gathered around her to protect her from all sides, but her silence sends a shiver through me. My eyes lock on Eric's, and he mirrors my concern. I see him dart his gaze in her direction while keeping the demons in sight.

Something is not right.

"I'm a demon." Colt saunters to join Satanael. "How about you come sniff me? You might even like it." A few of the demons blocking our path snicker until their leader glares at them.

"If you need some angel scent to mix it up, I'll come along with him." Worries about Helena can wait, so I move closer.

"Ask who sent them," Helena's murmured question is loud enough for me to barely hear it.

Many questions come to mind. Could it be that someone else took Abaddon's place that fast? Was this some trap the jinn had ready for us if we stepped inside this realm? If the latter was true, Helena's life might still be in danger, so we have to focus on that instead of chasing things that may not be true.

"I will rip you limb from limb." Satanael, ever the impatient, takes a step forward, and I grab for him to hold him back. "Remove your hand, Raphael, so I don't remove it for you."

"They are not worthy of any discussion, Samael." Taking Helena's lead, I cock my head when he glares at me. "They should bring whoever sent them to speak with you. You are a ruler of Hell, after all. You don't negotiate with lowly scum."

"Someone sent them?" Even I flinch when his features sharpen and his body grows before my eyes. "Who is your master, scum?" He rounds on the demons who are cowering at his power. "Let me help him understand there can only be one lord all of you answer to in this realm."

"We heard you were a prisoner, my lord," the talkative idiot hisses, saying the title mockingly. "With Lucifer gone, it's every demon for themselves now. Hand us the angel and the girl. You are outnumbered."

Another dozen or so demons show themselves from behind the trees, joining the line already facing us. Anger prickles inside me, the feeling of it so much different than anything I felt before entering Purgatory that it takes my breath away. Rolling my shoulders, I try to loosen the tensed muscles on my back, but that only irritates me more.

"I think you need to learn some manners." With that casually thrown comment, Colt pounces on the demon closest to him.

Hoots and roars echo in the open space when the demons descend on us. Samael plows through a handful of them as his wings snap open, his claws raking deep gauges through their bodies. My own wings spread wide, and I dare not glance at them in case any changes have occurred. I keep my focus on the hellspawn who dares threaten Helena after everything all of us have gone through to keep her alive. Colt, Samael, and I hold back the idiots daring to face not just Helena's father to get to her, but Beelzebub, Lucifer's sons, and me.

Black blood splatters the dirt under our feet, making if harder to move without slipping on it. Weight placed on the balls of my feet, I twist and turn to avoid arms grabbing for my wings, my fists crunching bones and caving skulls. Screams join our infuriating snarls, and among them, I hear her.

Helena.

My arm is nearly ripped from my body when I turn to

find her in the middle of the fight. Shaking the pesky demon off me, I rush to get near her in case she needs my help. I shouldn't worry since Eric doesn't move from her side, but I can't help myself. Stumbling, I trip on my own feet when I see her scream and grab for her shoulder, but I see no one close enough to touch her. *Maybe they are throwing weapons*, I tell myself to stove off panic. Why is she hurting?

"Angel, either fight or go away." Eric grunts and rips a demon's head. "Don't just stand there and look pretty."

"You okay?" Helena huffs before she darts forward and stabs another hellspawn on the neck without blinking an eye. "Raphael?"

"Are you hurt?" As soon as I blurt it out, I regret it.

Eric spins around, snatching her in his arms, and I rush after him toward the back of the fight. Mutely, I watch as he runs his hands over her to check for an injury, but I can't look away from her shoulder. There is no blood or marks on it. My own throbs where the demon yanked on it hard, and the pain dulls when I see her pressing her fingers on the same spot on her body. A tremor passes through me, yet I can't understand what is going on.

"I'm fine, Eric." She slaps his hands away with a scowl. "Will you stop?"

"Where did you see her hurt?" Lucifer's son rounds on me.

"I was wrong." I shrug, my eyes still locked on Helena's hand pressed on her shoulder.

"Ladies, are you going to fight, or did you chip a nail?" Colt's voice reaches my ears from a few yards behind us.

"I'm going to kill myself," Helena groans, and I can't help but smile. "I lived to hear that dumbass call me a coward." With a roll of her eyes, she walks around Eric and tugs me along when she passes me. "Let's go show them how it's done, Raphael." A wide smile pulls her lips up, and she turns to wink at me. "Play time, motherfuckers."

It comes naturally to follow her, not just for me but for Eric as well. Her laughter bounces around as the three of us dash into the fray of bodies mashed together in a pile of kicks and fists. Helena's tail flicks behind her every time she spins, and when she nears Satanael, it's a beauty to watch them side by side.

Say what you want about the King of Wrath, but when his daughter is beside him, his full focus is on her wellbeing. While the number of demons dwindles and the rest of us make quick work of them, father and daughter dance in sync like they've done this for millennia.

Samael is a whirlwind of claws and wings around her, while she literally throws our attackers on her dagger. With a fierce expression, she stabs and cuts before moving to the next. The four of us gather in a group when only two are left, and we can't look away from the end of the fight. Helena's hair falls over her face when she slices the neck of the last demon and, panting, she and Samael grin at each other.

"Well. I'll be damned," Beelzebub grumbles under his breath for our ears only. "I never thought Samael cared about anything but himself, offspring or not."

"She has that effect on everyone, does she not?" Pride swells inside me just watching her victorious. "Not even the Devil himself is immune to that."

"That's my mate you're talking about, Archangel. I'd hate to pluck your feathers one by one," Eric snarls from next to me, but there is no heat in it.

Helena turns her head to smile at us, and a hush falls over our group.

"Let's get her out of here."

With that, Eric saunters with purpose, swiping her in his

arms. Samael shakes his head at the possessive display but follows them without a word. We are on their heels as well when unease prickles inside me. Especially when she looks over Eric's shoulder and her eyes land on my still sore shoulder. Did she see me get hurt? Is that why she is checking? Because we had the same injury, or is there something more to it?

Purgatory is still messing with my mind. I'm imagining things.

That must be it, because the alternative is too frightening to consider.

Chapter Eight

ERIC

"You will not pass, Shadow." The damn Haltija puffs up his narrow chest, blocking my way to the bedroom. My bedroom, nonetheless.

"Step out of my way, Narsi I know Helena is there."

For some stupid reason, I agreed not to hurt the Haltija, and now the little shit thinks it's okay to stand between me and my mate. After we returned from Hell with Satanael in tow, we spread out to collect whatever we may need for our trip. According to Helena's father, our search should start from the outskirts of Atlanta and go up north to Maine. From the few things he remembers while he was kept prisoner, the jinn liked to keep their celestial hostages on Earth. Not a bad idea if you ask me, since neither Heaven nor Hell will think to look among the humans for their missing residents. It's not a far stretch to expect my father or Michael to go on a quest of their own making and return decades later. If the jinn didn't go after Helena, no one would've noticed something had bee amiss for centuries.

That information doesn't sit well with my mate. The fact

that her mother has been close while she thought her dead fans the anger and guilt she forces upon herself, and it just makes everything worse. I hope it'll be easier on her if she talks it out, but that backfires big time. The more she explains what's been going through her head, the more she withdraws from all of us.

From me more than the rest.

I never want to use our bond to bend her to see my perspectives, but as I had once proven, I have the means to achieve that. Helena can be as angry as she wants, but she can't control the reaction her body has to my touch. Shamelessly, I have every intention of using sex to bring my Helena back. The feisty firecracker who shot me to prove a point. I thought she just needed time to process everything after being snatched by the Fates, but I was wrong. Her fire is buried under all the unnecessary weight that's not hers to carry, and all I have to do is just fan the flames.

I'm more than happy to do that.

"My Mistress does not wish to be disturbed." Narsi's eyeless sockets narrow to slits. "If you force me, I will eat your face."

"You can't eat faces, and Helena told you this." With a sig,h I watch his small shoulders slump dejectedly. "And I don't want to hurt you because she cares about you. So, unless you are planning to grow to full size, which will bring this house down and harm her in the process, get out of my way."

"I don't like you, Shadow." The hiss is full of venom.

"Likewise, spirit. Now move." As I push my way past him, I slam the door in his face.

My gaze finds Helena immediately, and the sight of her tightens my chest. She sits in the middle of the bed with her knees pulled to her chest and her cheek pressed on them.

Lost in her thoughts, her eyes—although open—see things none of us can. Whatever memories fill her mind are not pleasant if the look on her face is anything to go by. It gives me a pause long enough to debate if I should approach her or go find Cass. Maybe her human friend can be of more help to my mate.

"Are they ready to leave?" Her voice is raspy, which tells me she hasn't spoken since our conversation with Satanael.

"Not yet." Throwing caution to the wind, I join her on the bed. My fingers graze the side of her face, and her eyes flutter shut. "It will be best if we leave at first light instead of now, I think."

"Did something happen?"

"No, but we can all use the rest." Her gaze flicks to my face at my comment. "All of us have been cleaning up the city as best as we can. Muscling halfway across the country is no problem, but we do need to strategize too if we do find any jinn."

"I think we won't find any jinn." Her head lifts, and she turns to face me. "The Fates destroyed whatever was left of them when I made the deal."

"To be the balance." It's not a question, yet she nods regardless.

"Listen Eric, I ..." Hel gnaws on her lower lip, and I tug it out from under her teeth with my thumb. "Umm, maybe I didn't exactly tell you everything the Fates said to me."

"Okay, I'm all ears." Plucking her off the bed, I settle with my back to the headboard and place her in my lap. "Take your time. This may take a while."

"Well"—She shivers when my hands glide up her arms and over her shoulders—"I don't really have a choice in what I could or couldn't agree with ... whatever is shoved at me."

"Mhmm." Nuzzling her exposed throat, I start pressing featherlight kisses up to her ear and back, flicking my tongue in the spot where her neck meets the shoulder. "No choice, got it." My lips graze her skin, and it pebbles from the brush of it. "What else?"

"They wanted to take something from me I was not willing to give." My mate tilts her head to the side, and I can't stop the smile at seeing the submissive pose.

The brush of my lips turns into open-mouthed kisses, and Helena groans, her fingers latching onto my shoulders. Taking advantage of that, I wrap my hand in her hair to hold her in place as the tip of my tongue travels from her clavicle, up her neck, and around her jawline. Nuzzling her cheek with mine, my cock jumps when she sighs, and her hips jerk forward to press harder on it. Slowly, I bring our mouths closer until the corners graze hers, and then I flick my tongue there, making her squirm.

"I know what you are doing." The accusation is mute because she is gyrating on my lap and driving me insane.

"Is it working?" Pulling back, I lock my gaze on hers and smirk when I see how dilated her pupils are.

"I'll tell you in a minute, keep going." She grabs a fistful of my hair and jerks my head back. "But I think you are wearing too many clothes."

Her mouth crushes on mine, and without missing a beat, I spear my tongue inside it. Like a starving male, I devour her, sucking, nipping, and licking every space I can reach. Helena wraps around me tight, pushing her core on my erection, and I can feel the heat coming from her warming me through the fabric of my pants. Taking hold of her ass with both hands, I grind her on me, and the low moan nearly makes me spill like a pubescent boy. Her unique-to-her scent fills my nostrils, and I can barely hold

onto the control I have so I don't rip whatever she is
wearing to shreds.

"I could say the same for you, Hel." Panting as I come
up for air, I nip at her swollen lips. "I'll fix that little problem
we have, but you can continue telling me what you haven't
shared with me yet."

"Okay." She nods enthusiastically and scrambles off me
so I can start undressing her. "I can't remember what I was
saying."

It soothes my male ego that my mate reacts readily to
any contact with me, and I'm not ashamed to grin at her
dazed state when I slide to the edge of the bed and pull her
to stand between my legs. I run my hands over her sides and
her breasts, molding them between my fingers until she
throws her head back and silently demands for more.
Giving my claws an inch of space to come out, I hook them
under the seam of her shirt and rip a straight line up her
spine, tugging it off her with a flick of my wrist. When I
latch onto her erect nipple and suck hard, her mewling fuels
my urgency to be inside her, so I make quick work of her
pants too.

"I can never get enough of seeing you naked." She
struggles when I hold her at arm's length to look my fill.
"Are we back to being ashamed when I look at you?"
Her gaze drops, and I duck my head, searching for it
until she looks me in the eye. "You don't believe me
when I say you are the most beautiful female I have ever
seen?"

"We both know I'm not." One corner of her mouth
cocks into a wry grin.

"To me you are." Hooking a crooked finger under her
chin, I lift her face up. "That's all that matters, because if
another male wants to have you like this, I will rip him into

so many pieces Heaven and Hell won't be able to put him together."

"You really mean that." Her green gaze darts between mine.

"Do you know why you are the most beautiful, Hel?" When her head shakes, I let her see everything I feel for her in my own hungry gaze. "Because you are mine. Only mine."

Everything to this point was worth it just to see the smile blossoming on her pretty face. Her small hand cups my cheek, and I sigh as I turn and place a kiss on the center of her palm.

"You are mine too, Eric, and I think you are still way too dressed for this."

Helena squeals when I yank her off her feet and throw her on the bed in one move. Her lips part when I stand to face her, reaching back tugging the t-shirt over my head. "That's something I can fix immediately."

As soon as my pants hit the floor, I descend on her like a male possessed.

Chapter Nine

HELENA

Eric's hands all over me mess with my head, and I have to struggle to think. Maybe if I kept my mouth shut I could enjoy his naked body pressed over mine from shoulder to groin, but I had to blab shit out. His mouth travels down my neck and chest, the tip of his tongue swirling over my exposed, sensitive skin. Thrashing my head from side to side, I reach for him, my fingers kneading his back and shoulders with mad urgency.

"You were telling me something, Hel," he mutters over my nipple, his lips grazing the tender peak with each word. "Let's hear what you've been hiding." The wetness of his tongue swirls around the hard tip.

"Later." I pant, shifting my legs so his cock can press harder between my lower lips. "Less talking, more fucking."

"Is that so?" Eric chuckles and nips my nipple.

With a gasp, I claw at his shoulders. "Don't be a jerk. I need you."

"I have every intention of giving you everything you need until you can't stand on your feet, but I need to hear what you want to tell me first." Hips swiveling excruciatingly slow, he lifts his head to lock gazes with me. "Tell me."

I crush my mouth on his and dive in to kiss him hard enough for him to forget about talking. A groan rips from his chest and takes over until my head is full of cotton and my body full of need. Twisting my fingers in his hair, I want to pull him so close we are one being, until I can't tell where he ends and I begin. With all the turmoil choking me, I haven't had quality time with my mate because I did everything to avoid him. It all hit me the moment he started kissing me.

Eric's hard erection is gliding over my wet folds, the tip of his cock bumping the swollen button on each upward thrust. It sends zings of pleasure through me, and I mewl in his mouth, desperate to have him inside me. He is just as much in need of the connection judging by the drumming of his heart I can feel where my breasts are pressed to his chest. It beats in sync with mine like a techno beat between us.

"I want to feel you squeeze my cock while I'm as deep inside you as I possibly can be. So, start talking, Hel, for both our sakes." When he comes up for air, the order is pushed through his clenched teeth.

"Umm," I have to blink a few times to remember my name much less what we were talking about. "When the Fates had me pulled in whatever that place was"—To my disappointment, his hips stop moving—"she, they, it … whatever it was told me that I will lose you." Fresh tears prickled the back of my eyes, throwing cold water on my libido.

"I'm right here, my love." His lips brush against mine gently. "They'll have to drag my dead carcass away to pry me from you."

"That's the thing." My hold on him tightens. "I was told you or Raphael had to die, and I fought it."

"Of course you did, my little hellion." Love sparkles in his green gaze as the corners of his mouth curl up.

"Yeah, well, since I had no intention of giving you or him up to die, I was told I'll lose my powers." A deep sigh make the locks of hair that fall over his forehead rustle. "Which I was more than happy to part with, to be honest."

"What did you do, Hel?" Eric lifts on his elbows and watches me warily.

"You must know that I will always chose you over whatever magic I have, Eric." Huffing in annoyance, I glare at him. "Are you serious right now?"

"Obviously you'd do the same for the angel, but we can get back to that." Bracketing my head between his palms, he forces me to keep eye contact. "What did you do, Helena?"

"If you must know, being ready to give up my powers is apparently a good thing." My chin juts out stubbornly. Like hell I will apologize for keeping both of them alive. "So, I got to keep them since I was willing to part with them. A plus was the two of you still being around as well."

He stares at me.

"What?" This went to shit real fast.

"That's not all of it." The unreadable expression on his face sets me on edge, and I squirm a little under the penetrating gaze. "What else happened?"

"You know, Eric, I normally love it when you are naked, but you're killing that mood right now." If I think that will help me get away without spilling what I stupidly started, I am so wrong it's not even funny.

He enters me so suddenly a scream is dragged from my throat. My channel pulses around the steel of his cock, and my hips jerk up involuntarily to grind on his pelvis. Eric wraps his calloused fingers around my shoulders to pin me under him, but he doesn't move. No matter how much I wiggle and try to flop around, I can't move an inch.

"What else?" His strained tone tells me he is not as unaffected by it as he wants me to believe. "I can have you on my cock for as long as it takes, Helena, and you know this."

Oh boy, don't I fucking know it? Eric has enough stamina to keep going until I literally pass out mid-orgasm, and I have no doubt he will torture me for days like this until I tell him what he wants to know. For a crazy moment, I actually debate keeping my mouth shut. I mean, it's not like I'm suffering having him inside me. It actually feels really, *REALLY*, nice.

But, I need him to move.

"For my willing sacrifice, I got to keep my powers and have both of your lives tied to mine." It all came out in one mushed-together breath even I can barely understand. But Eric hears.

Oh, yeah. Hell forbid he misses that part.

"Tied how?" In fascination, I watch a muscle spasm on one side of his jaw. "Tied to you how, Helena?"

"I don't know, okay? All I cared about at the time was getting away from that creepy thing and making sure you two were still breathing when I did." I swallow thickly when his eyes narrow to slits. "I remember hearing that Raphael will be tied to my life and you'll be tied to my heart. After that, I was threatened that I must uphold the balance, or my life will belong to the Fates."

"I am your mate, so I'm already tied to your heart," he muses under his breath, searching my face for who knows what?

"I told you it was stupid. I just thought the mate bond was a soul connection, you know?" My lips purse in annoyance. "So, hearing you are tied to my heart kinda sounded more like a threat. I die, you die type of thing, which I'm not happy about, just so we are clear. Have you seen all the motherfuckers gunning for my head?"

Eric grins like I just told him he will be a father.

What in the actual fuck?

"You are smiling." I frowned, and his grin grew. "Why are you smiling? Stop that. It's freaking me out."

"This is wonderful news." He kisses all logic out of my brain. "I'm not happy about the whole Raphael thing, but this is amazing."

"You are seriously creeping me out." My huffing sounds too loud when I try to catch my breath. "I couldn't sleep because I didn't know how to tell you this, and you're happy about it?"

"Oh, yes." The tilt of his mouth will tell anyone that Eric is Lucifer's son. It's devilish and full of mischief. "I feared I would have to chain you in the basement to keep you alive because you, my little mate, have absolutely no self-preservation skills. The Fates have given me a gift."

"You are not making sense. I'm just saying."

"You'll throw your life away without a second thought if you think it'll protect those you care about, but this changes everything." I want to punch him when he chuckles in glee. "If you die, Raphael and I will follow." Chortling in my face, he shakes his head. "This will stop you from your suicidal tendencies because you want us alive."

"I fail to see how all this is funny, jackass." When shoving on his shoulders doesn't move him away, I give up on that idea. "What do you expect me to do? Hide when human lives are on the line? It defies the purpose of protecting them."

"You'll need another plan instead of going head-first into danger," he informs me happily and pecks me on the lips. "It's quite brilliant, actually."

"Right, because nothing sounds better than all three of us dying at once." Whatever else I want to say is gone when he starts moving his hips.

Heaven, Hell, Fates … all of them together can smack me on the head for all I care.

Eric is merciless when he is focused on my body.

Chapter Ten

ERIC

I can't look away from Helena's face when I pull out until just the tip of my cock is inside her before plunging back in to the root. Her channel spasms, trying to keep me inside her to no avail when I start pumping my hips. The happiness makes my arms tremble, and her words repeat in a loop inside my head.

I know my mate better than she knows herself. With us tied to her life, there is no way she'll be reckless. The memory of the recant fight, case and point, explains why she held back instead of pouncing on the demons the second they were in sight.

My hips keep a steady rhythm, sinking me inside her heat and drenching my thighs with her wetness. I take her in while she writhes under me, from the strands of blonde hair spread around her head like a golden cloud to the place where we are joined. Her breasts bounce every time I bottom out, luring me to suck the hard nipples between my teeth.

"God yes." Her nails drag down my back as her head thrashes from side to side.

"I don't think he has anything to do with it, love." Panting, I increase the tempo, the sounds of skin slapping skin filling my ears.

"Harder, Eric," Hel mewls, clawing at me and tightening her thighs around my waist. "Faster."

My head bows, and I take her nipple between my lips, swirling my tongue around it. My abdominal muscles clench tight like a rock when the position changes the angle of my cock, the mushroom head sinking deeper inside her. Helena shrieks, tilting her pelvis higher, and she bucks hard of the mattress in an attempt to reach the elusive high we are nearing. My testicles tighten painfully the more she swivels her hips, and a tingle starts at the base of my spine.

Like a wild animal, I root over my mate, insatiable and almost feral. My upper lip curls over my teeth from the need to possess her completely, and no matter how deep I am inside her body, it never seems like it's enough.

"Say it." My snarl pebbles her skin with gooseflesh. "Say it, Hel."

My mate gives as good as she gets, but instead of voicing the words I need to hear, she smirks at me, her half-lidded gaze daring me to make her obey me. It feeds the insanity overtaking my mind every time I take my mate, and I start smacking my hips with a punishing strength between her legs. Her back bows off the bed, almost dislodging me off her.

If she thinks I'm too gone to remember what I asked she will be sorely mistaken. Wrapping one arm around her waist, I tug her off the mattress and flip us around. Her golden hair falls over her shoulders and around my head like a waterfall, the red tiny horns peeking through it.

Without missing a beat, her ass bounces on top of my groin, sinking me forever deeper in her heat. I wrap my fingers over her ass cheeks, squeezing and helping her pump up and down faster on my cock.

"Helena," Her name is pushed through my teeth in a warning.

"Eric," she moans my name, stubbornly denying me.

My hand connects with her ass with a loud smack, the flesh quivering from the slap. She gasps, and a new torrent of wetness gushes out of her pussy, drenching the top of my thighs. It feeds the crazed need I have for her, so I do it again. And again, until the skin warms under my hand. The whole time she bounces faster and harder, impaling herself on my hardness with frantic movements.

"Say it, Hel." My voice sounds off to my own ears. Otherworldly. Feral. "I will not let you cum until you say it."

"Asshole." My mate pants, her nails digging into my chest.

Seeing this is not giving me what I want more than anything, so I flip us around again, this time pulling out of her completely. Her protests and threats echo around us until I turn her around, lifting her ass in the air and sinking inside her with one hard thrust. The quivering flesh before me has a red handprint where my palm connected with it, and the tingling in the base of my spine intensifies. Anchoring her with one hand on her hip, I wrap my fingers around her hair and tug it back until she can almost see me if she looks up.

"Say it."

"Yours," Hel screams, pushing back for all she is worth. "I'm yours."

All rational thought leaves my mind, and I piston fast enough that my groin and thighs are stinging from the force of it. Helena's deep, guttural moans mix with my snarls in the otherwise silent room. Not a second too soon, her channel clenches around me so tight I can't keep pumping inside her. And I explode. My cock swells and jerks, spurting stream after stream into my mate. Bright lights and stars dance behind my closed eyelids, and I shake on my feet while my roar rattles the windows of the room. Helena's scream and incoherent words join it.

After what feels like a split second and an eternity later, she goes limp in my arms, and I sag over her, my forehead pressing between her shoulder blades. The jackknifing of my heart matches hers as we both gasp for air, thoroughly spent. Sweat covers our bodies, and our skin sticks everywhere we touch while I press featherlight kisses any place I can reach.

"Holy shit, Eric," my mate huffs, turning her head to the side so I can kiss along the line of her jaw. "That was—"

"The best orgasm you've ever had?" My words are muffled and raspy.

"I was going to say amazing, but sure, let's go with that." She laughs weakly, shaking her head at me. "We don't want your arrogant ass to get a pin and explode your head now, now do we?"

My chuckle is rewarded with a carefree giggle. I haven't heard her laugh like this since we returned to the human realm, and it loosens the tightness in my chest. Keeping my cock still inside her, I lift Hel in my arms and stretch out on the bed, holding her to my chest. She wiggles slightly before settling, and a sigh puffs out from her swollen lips. I brush her hair off the side of her face with my chin and press us cheek to cheek.

"I love you." I suck in a deep breath, filling my lungs

with her scent. Well, our scent to be exact, which fills the room with both of us and the musky tinge of sex.

"I love you too, Eric." Hel's voice cracks with emotion. "So much."

My arms tighten around her.

"Listen, I know that for whatever reason, what I said earlier it makes you happy. Knowing you, it's probably some arrogant male ego thing you have going on, but that's not important." She rasps her nails over my arm. "Your and Raphael's lives being tied to mine presents a bit of a problem."

"I fail to see this problem, love." Eyes closing, I enjoy the gentle scratching she does over my forearm. "All I can think of is the fact that you won't be rushing head-first into a fight anymore. Not if you know that anything happening to you will affect us. As much as I admire that you care so much, sometimes I think you do so more for others than yourself."

"Wow, I did not see that one coming." Her dry tone told me she did in fact expect to hear those exact words.

I frown.

"Let me enlighten you so I can screw up your post-sex bliss." With a strained chuckle, she stops scratching my skin. "It's not that it only affects the two of you if I get hurt. You see, if the two of you dumbasses jump in to protect me like you are known to do and you get injured in the process"— Dread spread through me in a wave—"I am injured too."

Hel is as stiff as a board in my arms, and I'm wound up so tight I can break in half if I try to move a muscle. The need to find the Fates and rip them limb from limb is so overwhelming I jerk away from my mate, my cock protesting when it slides out of her heat. Jumping off the bed, I start pacing back and forth, my fingernails scraping my scalp.

"No," I spit out in anger. "No fucking way, Hel. We need to find the Fates and fix this." The room feels too small, and there is not enough air to fill my lungs.

Helena turns around, propping her head on one hand to watch me pace. "Did I tell you how pretty your cock is?" She wiggles her eyebrows. "Like really pretty. Picture worthy."

That freezes me for a second before I glare at her. "This is not a fucking joke."

"I'm not joking, Eric. I'm dead serious." She gives me a pointed stare at the still-hard erection bobbing at my groin. "Beautiful."

"Get dressed. We need to talk to Raphael." Finding my pants, I snatch them, stabbing my feet in the legs.

Helena shakes her head but doesn't argue. We dress in silence while I try my best not to lose my shit. In the back of my head, I am well aware of how big of a hypocrite this makes me, but I have no time to dwell on dumb shit. Hel is in more danger this way than any other time since the jinn decided to fuck with us.

I'll be damned if I let them take my mate without doing everything I can to stop them. The feathered prick better help me in this, or I'll pluck his wings.

Fates or not, they can be killed, too. I hope.

Chapter Eleven

HELENA

I learned that when Eric gets adamant about something, I have two options in dealing with him: stand back and let him exhaust himself before I maneuver him in the direction I need him to go or threaten to stab him. The latter worked like a charm most of the time. He still remembers when I shot him in the ass when we first met. Okay, fine, it was the upper thigh.

Definitely one of my finest moments, if I can say so myself.

Pulling the dagger from the sheath strapped to my thigh, I scrape the tip under my nails and watch him shout from the top of his lungs for the Archangel. Narsi darts around the corner, skidding to a stop where I'm leaning on the wall and latches onto my leg koala style, his head flicking back and forth between us.

"Shadow makes Narsi angry." My sidekick bares his yellowed teeth, his empty eye sockets scrunched in frustration. "I will eat his face."

"No, you won't." Snorting, I pet the top of his unruly

curls, and he leans into my touch like an excited puppy. "We said no eating the faces of anyone in this house, remember?" The reminder makes him pout, but he smoothes his tiny hand over the shirt he is wearing.

Eric bellows down the hall, "Raphael. I know you're there, so get your feathered ass in the common room. Now."

I don't point out that technically both of them are feathered pains in my ass. My attention is drawn to Narsi's shirt and the golden feather pinned like a broach on his chest. The same one he found when the Fates pulled us into their own space, which fell from my wings. The childlike fingers grazed it gently, reverently, like something of great importance had been bestowed upon him.

My shoulder blades tingle.

"He is ignoring me on purpose." Eric stomps toward me, his fists balled at his sides. "And you"—His finger points at Narsi, making my sidekick's upper lip curl over yellowed teeth—"stay out of my way today, or I will kick you back to Hell before you have a chance to fight me on it."

Narsi's head tilts up slowly, and he turns his face toward mine, where I'm looking down at him. "Can I eat him now?" It takes everything in me not to bark out a laugh at his pleading expression.

"Not yet." Head cocked to the side, I give Eric a pointed look and a smirk. "Depending on how today goes, I might let you do it later, though."

With a shake of his head, Eric spins on his heel, his yell making me flinch. "Raphael, Helena is hurt."

My mouth opens to call him out on his lie, but I'm too late. Multiple pairs of feet create a thundering stampede headed our way from two directions. Colt, Beelzebub, and George rush from our left, and Satanael, with Raphael and Cass on his heels, dart from the right. All of them skid to a halt when they see me propped on the wall with Narsi wrapped around my leg, while Eric stands in the middle of the hallway, his hands on his hips and a grin plastered on his lips.

I snicker and proceed to clean under my nails with the dagger.

"Oh, great. All of you are here, so I don't have to go looking." Eric sneers, his anger directed mostly at the Archangel. "It's almost as if you knew I needed to talk to all of you."

Narsi chortles like a deranged person.

"I should've known my brother was having a tantrum and using his mate to get attention," Colt spits between clenched teeth. "Some of us need to gather what we require for our trip. We can't sit around to chat."

It's obvious they are all upset, and an argument is about to explode in the tight space. Knowing them, there will be fists flying too, something I'm really not in the mood for. Mind spinning in search of something to say to defuse the situation, whatever is ready to come out of my mouth is stuck in my throat. Face twisted in fury, Eric points an accusing finger at my face.

"She will die if Raphael and I are killed. One of us not surviving an injury will cost Helena her life."

The silence is oppressive.

Seven pairs of hard eyes and one pair of empty eye sockets pin me to the wall. My nervous laugh doesn't help, but I lift my hands in surrender, inching as close to the nearest door as I can. "It's actually not as horrible as he makes it sound." Narsi drops his legs on the ground and digs his heels in to prevent me from moving.

Eric is lucky we just had sex. There will be no tumble in the sheets in his near future for doing this to me. If he knows he's up to his earlobes in shit, he will be groveling instead of glaring at me like I just spit in his cereal. Asshole.

"Helena?" Raphael's tone is low and full of horror when he steps around Satanael's large frame. "Is this true?" His golden eyes bore into mine, speeding my heart rate to alarming levels. "Back in the village where we found your father. My shoulder … I thought, but it cannot be."

A muscle is quivering in my jaw.

"Someone better starts explaining. What are you talking about, Raphael?" Satanael grabs the Archangel, yanking him around to face him. "Stop blabbering like a fool and say what is on your mind. What does your limb have to do with my daughter?" he demands.

Eric puffs up, and I make sure he knows I'll stab him later for this. "I'll deal with you later." With a sigh, I press more of my weight on the wall. "We don't know for sure that your injuries can kill me, for one. Second, what any of this means for us is all a guessing game, for now."

"One of the demons latched onto my arm, and as I turned, it wrenched it out of its socket." Great, I guess they are going to act like I'm not standing right here. "Helena was rubbing hers in the same spot, and she was favoring the same arm. I did not see her receiving any blows in the fight."

All six males start talking at once, trying to outshout one another. It's surprising to see George getting in Eric's face, most of all since my hunter friend has been getting more accustomed to all the creatures of Hell and Heaven prowling around him lately. He didn't watch Underworld inhabitants with disgust anymore, but right now, hatred burned in his irises.

"Not a boring day around here, amirite?" Cass bumps

her shoulder on mine, ignoring the cluster of red-faced males crowding the hallway.

"This is called 'fuck you very much Helena' for making sure all of us survived the jinn," I tell her with a cheerfulness I don't feel. My arm is raised so I'm ready to snatch Narsi at any given moment if he goes for someone's face.

He looks too perky.

"Is it true, though?" My friend peers at me, a cloud of bouncy chestnut curls dancing around her shoulders. "Anyone can hurt you by stabbing one of them?"

I purse my lips, giving her a side-eye. Colt bares his teeth at his twin in a macabre smile, while Satanael's vein is throbbing on one side of his temples. Beelzebub, with his tree-trunk arms crossed over his chest, has Raphael pinned under his red-glowing glare, and George is poking my mate with an insistent finger at the center of his chest.

"I think so," I admit to her under my breath before speaking louder. "But to find out for sure, I'm willing to start stabbing at all of them. Then I'll know which of them bleeding affects me the most."

The annoying buzz of many voices disappears, and they all turn toward me, mouths slightly open. With a grin, I twirl my dagger between my fingers. My father isn't worried about my threat, but he does take it personally.

"This isn't the time for humor, daughter." Shoulders squared, he lifts to his full height, the arrowhead tip of his tail twitching behind him. "If what Lucifer's son says is true, he and the Archangel will have to stay back and always be close to you. I will not have them on the front lines only to lose my flesh and blood for their incompetence."

As predicted, the two males he just named useless in a fight speak together, calling him a prick and telling him they are willing to demonstrate how good of a warrior each of them is. My father's lips curled in a freakish expression that told my monkey brain to run screaming and hide. Cass, leaning against the wall next to me, jolts, so I place a fingers on her forearm to tell her she's safe. Satanael wouldn't dare to hurt my friend. If he tries, I'll cut off his tail. And the horns.

"Enough." My bark brings a much-needed silence, and I grab for Narsi, wrapping my fingers in the back of his shirt to jerk him back when he pounces. "If you move an inch from my leg, I'll saw your mouth shut, and then you won't be eating any faces any time soon. How about that?"

Pouting, he shrinks back and glowers, peeking at me with one eye socket from around my leg.

"You"—The tip of my blade stabs the air at Satanael— "will still be chained if the two you just called incompetent didn't find you. So, how about you stop insulting them. And most importantly, there won't be much fighting going on now that the jinn are gone, so let's not worry who will jump first to throw fists, huh?"

A strange expression fleets over my father's face, and my heart stutters when I notice the same on Raphael's. The rest stiffen as well, and pregnant tension drops over us heavy enough to make my knees buckle.

"We received a word." Raphael shifts on his feet.

Eric's chest rumbles.

"Stop growling, Eric." The sounds stop, and I lock my narrowed gaze on the Archangel. "Well?"

"After we returned with Satanael, we sent a message to everyone still prowling through the city in search of survivors." The Archangel exchanged a loaded glance with my father. "To ask anyone if they have noticed unusual activities around Atlanta. We just left the group of hunters when Eric called out. They said MARTA is definitely a place all of them avoid."

"The Atlanta metro? Why? Did the tunnels cave in?" My eyebrows dip low over my eyes. What does that have to do with anything?

"Terror made all of them turn around and walk away." Raphael watches me like a hawk to see my reaction.

Numbness spreads through me.

"Jinn." My lips don't move when I breathe that one word, and he gives me a sharp nod.

"It could be leftover wards they forgot to remove." George pitched in with no conviction in his tone.

My eyes slowly roll over everyone until they lock on Eric. "We can start the search there."

"Very well," my mate agrees, but my sigh of relief is short-lived. "Let's grab whatever we have ready. Beelzebub, Colt, George, and Satanael will take the lead. The three of us will take the back."

Like hell I'll take the back, but I keep my mouth shut. It's not easy to endure the heavy gaze Eric holds on me until my lungs start burning. My bright smile forms a line between his brows, too, but the rest dart in all directions, and he doesn't have time to lecture me. I grab Cass's hand and drag her toward the front door. With Maddison gone, all the responsibilities are on her shoulders for the safe house.

"You'll be careful, Hel. Promise me." My friend tightens her hold on my fingers.

"Always," I tell her, avoiding her piercing gaze, along with the guilt drowning me for forcing her to stay behind.

The dagger strapped on my thigh warms, reacting to my emotions, and my tail flicks, making my butt cheeks clench. I'll have time to feel bad later.

It's time for killing leftover scum, methinks.

Chapter Twelve

HELENA

George is not very happy to be carried like a duffle bag in Beelzebub's arm, but since the second option was being up close and personal with Colt, he keeps his mouth shut. I'm not ecstatic for my much-too-human friend to fight the jinn either—if there are any left in Atlanta—but he told me I had to give him this. Plus, who am I to judge if he wants to fight? I will just hide the fact that I ask Beelzebub and my father to keep an eye on him.

Better to be safe than sorry.

A cold wind pelts my skin as I wobble in the air. I'm still too weak to flap my wings like the rest of them, so I wave them up and down, keeping my formation by sheer will alone. Eric even agrees that my stubbornness proves very productive in this. Ass tight so I don't pitch toward the ground every time my tail brushes over it, I strain the new limbs as much as I can, repeating *"almost there"* like a mantra in my head.

Colt dips to the side, making a wide circle to join me at the back. "How you holding up, she-devil?"

"Peachy," I squeeze through clenched teeth.

Chuckling, he lifts above me, his wingspan casting a dark shadow over my body. Refusing to fall for his bullshit, I keep my eyes glued on the speck of land in the distance where we will enter the underground Atlanta metro network. It's easy to see it now that most of the skyscrapers are sliced in half as if God himself was pissed off and slashed a planet-sized sword across them. Sorrow weighs heavy in my chest, but I push it away.

Eric and Raphael have a heated discussion ahead of me, forgetting I can see them. My path to them is cut off when Colt glides a little too close for comfort, the feathers of his wings brushing mine and making me tilt sideways until I almost lose the current I'm riding.

"You know we won't be in the air forever, right?" My voice cracks from the panic choking me. "The second my feet touch the ground, I suggest you run, or it won't be jinn that kill you."

"Come now, Hel." Flipping over like he is swimming the backstroke, Eric's twin tucks his hands behind his head with an arrogant smirk. "Everyone is always so serious. A little fun won't harm anyone."

"Just me if I drop hundreds of feet to the ground," I mutter under my breath, and his grin grows. "You really are an asshole."

"Nah." He shrugs, and I want to jump on his stomach so he can drop and see how it'll feel. It pisses me off to see him so carefree while I'm sweating bullets. "I'm just trying to show you that flying is second nature for all of us. Not something you need to concentrate on so it works. The wings are part of you, and if you were not meant to fly, you wouldn't have them. Just relax."

All sarcasm washes off his face, and at times like this, he

looks so much like Eric it's freaky. After dealing with the jinn, anyone resembling someone I know sends my heart galloping in my chest. But this is Colt, and all his mockery aside, I know he won't hurt me, although I do keep my narrowed eyes on him longer than necessary.

"It's not a foreign thing you need to control. It's part of you." His voice is smooth, and the tension in my shoulders loosens slightly. "All you have to do is simply think where you want to be and let them do their thing. See yourself flying in the back of your mind to the destination. Then just breathe."

Raphael and Eric had taken turns teaching me how to use the feathered appendages, and his words were no different than the ones they'd repeated million times before. Yet, the fact that we might come across jinn in less than fifteen minutes made it more urgent to feel comfortable with my wings. Pressing my lips together, I gave Colt a determined nod.

With a deep breath, I close my eyes and relax, pressing my weight on the pressure of the breeze rustling my feathers. The tight band over my chest loosens, and I smile broadly as strands of my hair graze my shoulders and upper arms. Warmth spreads through me, melting the icy terror that had me in its grip the second my feet left the solid ground.

I open my eyes and grin wide at Colt before I notice him gaping at me.

He is bathed in a soft golden glow with specks of burnt orange, and his eyes are like saucers on his face. Mouth unhinged, he doesn't look like he is breathing, which makes my heart skip a beat, and I plunge toward the ground. Why did my wings fold on my back?

Flailing, my shriek echoes across the city while my ass

flips over my head, my tail writhing like the rope of a kite behind me. Panic claws and rakes my insides, and I grunt hard when my body is jerked up. A pair of strong arms tug me to a hard chest, but I can't see who catches me because my eyes are squeezed shut, though I cling to his shirt with the desperation of a drowning man. It takes a second for the train thundering in my ears to go away and for me to hear the person muttering soothing words. Shaking like a leaf, I lift my face with great effort and look up at Colt.

Eric's brother has never looked that pale. His green eyes stand out stark against his blanched face, and lines form deep groves around his firmly pressed mouth. Flicking his wide gaze over my head, he says something to whoever is behind me, but I don't dare turn around. Fuck moving, I'm going to glue myself to my mate's twin like white on rice until we are down on the ground. My fingers wrap harder around his shirt, the fabric protesting from my white-knuckled grip.

"What did you do to her," Eric's snarl penetrates my hysterical brain.

"I …" Colt darts a wary glance at me before locking it on Eric. "Nothing. She only tried to flip around. Let us … ummm … get where we are going first. I will carry her the rest of the way."

Like he has a choice.

If Colt tries to move his hands, I'm going to clamp my teeth on him and take off a chunk Narsi style before anyone can remove me from his hold. One time staring Death in the eye while flying is enough for me, thank you very much. Good thing Colt has never sounded so unsure since I've known him because Eric doesn't argue. Nor does he move away from us, flapping his wings so close the air tickles my exposed skin.

"We are almost there," Raphael chirps from our other side, telling me the Archangel didn't miss my embarrassment either.

"We can walk the rest." My voice is too high-pitched, but I couldn't care less. "Like, I'd love to stretch my legs."

Colt's arms tighten around me in a crushing hold. "No. We fly."

It's never too late to bite him, and it's actually very tempting, but he still has me in the air, and I'm scared to look down to see how high we are in the sky. That's the only thing saving Eric's twin from losing a chunk of meat right now. Quaking in my boots, I hug him the same way Narsi clings to me, spider-monkey style, arms and legs wrapped like bands around any part of his body I can reach.

"We will enter the metro at Five Points," Eric grumbles, and I'm grateful his voice soothes the crippling panic still rushing through me. "We will split up there; one group will follow south toward Atlanta airport through Oakland City. The other will search north to Sandy Springs through the Art Center."

I know what he is doing.

Sensing my distress, he rambles the same thing we agreed on before we left the safe house so he can take my mind off things. I focus on his words instead of imagining myself spiraling through the air to my death. As much as I'd love to brush it off, I keep thinking about why my wings folded the way they did. I sure as hell didn't want them to do that.

"We will meet back at Five Points if we find nothing." Raphael took over. "Then split up east and west if there is a need."

"We can go to Mars for all I care. Just take me to the

ground, please." My mumbling has all three of them groaning in agreement.

Before I know it, I jolt in Colt's arms, and we are on the ground. Scrambling off him, I drop on my knees, panting and running my hands over the grime like I just discovered the most precious treasure. A fist connecting to flesh has my head whipping around to see Colt sprawled on the floor and Eric looming over him.

"What the fuck did you do to her?" My mate snarls, hunching in preparation to pounce on his brother.

Lifting on his elbows, Colt zeroes in on me and gulps. "I did nothing, but her ..." Whatever color that has returned to his face drops away. "She glowed." His bulging eyes turn to Eric, and I remember him bathed in a weird light I thought was coming from somewhere behind me. "Heaven's light and Hell's magma made her skin, brother. I have never seen anything like it."

"Well, fuck a duck." My arms give out, and I drop on the pavement like a rock.

Chapter Thirteen

ERIC

"It means nothing." After I jump on the tracks from the platform, I reach for Helena. "It could be anything at this point."

We both know I'm trying to reassure myself more than her. That's why she says nothing and just takes my offered hand, following me to the metal rails where the metro used to zoom by daily until the jinn decided it was time for them to rule the realms. A long, dark tunnel stretches on both sides of us, and Hel shivers, wrapping her arms around her middle.

I curse up a storm under my breath.

What were we thinking? Both Raphael and I know what kind of personal hell my mate had in Purgatory, and like idiots, neither of us thought twice about bringing her here. My eyes lock on the Archangel, and I know he is thinking the same by the way his jaw is set and his knuckles white.

"You're right." Hel shrugs, peering intently at the black gaping hole of the tunnel. "And it's not like we can change anything, so what's the point of stressing about it. So, I glow. I also have wings, horns, and a tail. Big deal." An uneasy snort rasps out of her. "At least I don't have a third boob ... or a penis. Because let me tell you, if I grew one of those appendages, I have no doubt it would've been impressive in size, and I'd be chasing you right now with it bobbing ahead of me."

My chuckle makes her lips curl up, and it brightens her entire face. If threatening me with imaginary cocks makes her forget about all the unknown that scares her, I'll gladly suffer through it. Colt, on the other hand, can't wait for an opportunity to take a jab at me.

"You are not scaring him, she-devil. He likes it." My brother guffaws at my glare.

"We should've sent humans to search, not brought Helena here." Satanael peruses the underground terminal with his hands loosely propped on his hips.

"Of course." Helena sneers at him. "Because why send someone who's hard to kill when you can send humans, right? I have no clue why I didn't think of that."

"I do not care much for them." Poor Satanael is genuinely perplexed about why his daughter is upset with him.

"I couldn't tell." Muttering, she shuffles closer to me. "Can we go before I stab him in the forehead with the dagger?"

"We will meet you here in an hour." Beelzebub lifts a hand all business-like and trots toward the tunnel behind, followed closely by my twin and George. The hunter is a little green in the face, but he darts after them without a complaint. Satanael glances a few times at Hel, but my mates ignores him, so with a sigh and slumped shoulders, he disappears as well.

The sound of their thumping footsteps fades away.

"We should've brought the Trowe." Raphael steps on Helena's other side. "The wards are too strong in this place for them to have just missed it."

The short hairs on my arms standing at attention confirm he is telling the truth. Even from the sky, the deterrent placed around the tunnels under Atlanta prickled at my skin, warning me to get the hell away from the place. Deserted now after the attack, it has a creepy vibe to it even without the help of any warding, but the terror-inducing magic claws at my innards the longer I stand in one place.

"There is enough of us to deal with whatever is here." I still follow his gaze to where Helena is hyping herself to enter the tunnel.

I want for us to come across a jinn more than I ever wanted anything before. I need to rip into one of those pricks for doing this to my mate. For making a feisty, brave female wary of a fucking tunnel. My gums tingle where the sharp incisors want to drop so I can sink them in their necks and rip out their throats.

"The others will be back before we leave. Come on." Hel pulls out her dagger and, squaring her shoulders, steps forward.

Raphael and I follow on her heels, my arms tense and ready to grab her if she shows any signs of distress. A few feet in, it's already so pitch-black I can't see a finger if I lift it in front of my nose. Shifting my sight to my other form brings my surroundings into view, but I know neither the Archangel nor Helena can see in this darkness. I reach for my mate's arm to guide her, but before my fingers contact her skin, a soft glow forms a bubble around us.

Tilting my head, I stare at Raphael.

"A perk." One of his shoulders jerks in a shrug.

"Aww, look at you, Raphael." Hel giggles. "You are like a lightning bug."

"I'm not an insect." He sounds affronted, but I see his mouth twitching at the corners. "I'm an Archangel." A shadow crosses over his gaze, making me frown.

"Maybe I should try and see if I can do the same," Helena muses, and my attention goes back to her. I'll corner Raphael's angelic ass after we are done here to see what's up. "Knowing my luck, my boobs will light up like flashlights."

My bark of laughter echoes down the tunnel, and we all freeze.

"Very smooth, Eric," Hel says dryly. "Might as well send a marching band to announce our presence, why don't you?"

I shift my sight back to normal since I no longer need it and brush off the reprimand. At least she's no longer timid while walking in the claustrophobic space. Smooth concrete walls rise on both sides and form a rounded dome above our heads. The low railing lines a narrow path wide enough for one person to walk on, and so far, no door or entrance can be seen. Air heavy with the stench of heated metal and some type of gas coats my skin and the inside of my mouth.

The only sound is our breathing.

Hel's cargo pants cling to her legs and lush ass, pulling my gaze to the way each butt cheek wobbles with every step she takes. A sliver of skin is visible between her t-shirt and waistband, making my fingers twitch with the need to touch it. I would, too, if not for her tail flicking from side to side in a way that tells me she is not as relaxed as she wants me to believe.

"I don't think it's a bad sign," Raphael says out of nowhere.

"What's not a bad sign? That the tunnel is empty?" Confused, I give him a side-eyed glance.

"Her glow when she was flying." His chin tilts up, pointing at Helena's back.

"I would've asked what you think if you lit up like Christmas tree instead of me," Hel mutters and speeds up her footsteps.

"Hear me out," Raphael persists, and I bite the inside of my cheek so I don't cut him off.

I'm ready to kill anything and anyone to protect my mate, but how can I fight something I can neither see nor understand?

I stay silent.

"Zadkiel was …" He clears his throat when he chokes up. "Zadkiel is an Archangel, too. She can do almost everything I can, including casting a glow around herself. It stands to reason that you inherited some of her abilities, Helena."

"Lucky me," my mate mutters, but I know her attention is on every word coming out of the Archangel's mouth.

We pass one locked metal door with a heavy chain tightened to its limit around the doorknob.

"It is what I believe," Raphael pipes in with enough smoothness her head turns to give us a view of the side of her face, and she nods at him. "Also, Satanael commands the magma of Hell, does he not?"

I absently shake my head in confirmation, glancing around anything I can see for threats. An uneasy feeling pokes at me like we are being watched, but there is no one in the tunnels but us.

"I don't know where you're going with this, Raphael. I haven't seen my father leak any magma, and we were all in a fight together where we thought we were about to die. Remember?"

"I said he can control it. He is not Vulcan the Titan to leak magma through his orifices." A low chuckle rumbles in Raphael's chest.

I join him until Hel throws me a pointed glare.

My lips fold inward to stop me from laughing.

"And?" Hel snaps at the Archangel.

"I think now that your angel and demon parts are blended and brought to light, as they always should've been, you are adopting both powers to fit your specific needs." The deep tone is lulling and calming. Stupidly, I let it lower my alertness. "You are adjusting, that is all. You should not fear it."

"Maybe you are …" her words trail off, and I yank her behind me.

"Trolls." My snarl bounces off the walls, and my knees bend.

"Oh, shit," Hel breathes a second before a handful of eight-foot tall creatures with impenetrable skin fill up the tunnel.

Chapter Fourteen

HELENA

Tripping over one of the metal tracks, I stumble behind Eric when he practically throws me behind him. He and Raphael form a wall between me and the trolls, and crouch so I can see how many of them are there.

"Well, shit." I whispered on a shuddering exhale, trying to count the block-size heads when eight of those ugly motherfuckers' eyes meet mine.

"Helena, stay back," Raphael growls, hunching forward and preparing to fight.

"Go up the railing," Eric adds, his words only spiking my anger.

The dagger in my palm warms my damp skin. "I don't know if you two dumbasses forgot, but if any of them slaps your smug mugs, I'll feel it too. So how about you shove all your machoism up your arrogant asses, huh?" Shouldering my way between them, I place all my weight on the balls on my feet. "If anyone is going to use me as a punching bag, I'm going to make them bleed first."

Panic twists their faces, but I don't care. There is no way

I'm going to hide like some shrinking violet while others fight my battles. These brainless monsters were in *my* city terrorizing humans that are mine to protect. If they think I'll run like some little girl, all of them have another thing coming.

Eric curls his thumb and pinky over his lower lip, releasing a high-pitched whistle that rings in my ears. With the signal sent to the others—something they are hopefully close enough to hear—he jumps at the nearest troll. Claws lengthen on his fingertips, which he uses to instantly slash the creature's torso. If it was anything other than a troll, I'm sure his chest cavity would've been cracked like a walnut from it, but instead, the attack only leaves four deep slices, though at least he made the nasty bugger bleed..

A roar makes the walls around us shudder, and everyone moves at once while pebbles and dust rain over our heads. I try not to imagine the roof falling over us and burying us alive, but the imagine flutters through my mind nonetheless. With a dry mouth, I follow Eric, pouncing over him and landing on the first troll behind him, slashing my dagger at him. Lucky for us, these jerks are too big to crowd us all at once. They can only fit in the tunnel one at a time, and even then they have to twist their necks to the side to fit their heads.

Runes glowing bright, I filet the troll's chest to the bone, and the creature screams, the shrill force of it threatening to burst my eardrums. Dazed, I blink fast to clear my wavering vision when someone grabs my upper arm and plucks me away from my victim.

I shriek, but not in fear. In anger.

Without missing a beat, Raphael takes my place. Cocking his arm, he sinks it to his elbow inside the troll before he rips it out, his hand squeezing what looks like a palm-sized heart. The troll topples over then, knocking over the one behind him in the process. I'd call that a strike.

"Are you serious, Raphael?" Pissed, I scream at the Archangel's back. "I weakened him, just so you know. It was my fucking kill."

Ignoring me, he descends on the next creature stomping our way.

"Fuck you both," I huff in indignation, throwing both my hands in the air for added effect with so much strength the dagger nearly slips from my blood-covered hand.

Eric stands to the side of me, pummeling his troll into a bloody pulp. The creature's skull is as flat as a pancake, but he keeps at it like he wants to make sure it's *dead*, dead. Not just dead like a regular living being.

My tail curls tightly before it snaps out in rage.

With no intention of just standing there like a lump, I lean sideways to peer around Raphael and his troll, checking to see if I can possibly squeeze between them. All I need is the sliver of an opening, and I know I can wiggle my ass through to attack the next one lined up down the tunnel. How dumb are they to pick this tight, underground spot to crawl through, especially since they can barely fit in them? That thought gives me a pause. Even as stupid as they are, I'm pretty sure they don't want to be hunkered down in a place like this. I remember the two idiots I first saw dragging Narsi through Hell. Stupid, yes. Suicidal, not so much.

All wondering leaves my mind when I hear the chattering from behind me. With my heart lodged at the roof of my mouth, I spin on my heel, choking on empty air when I freeze in place. Dozens of rogue demons are crawling toward us like cockroaches, many of them climbing the walls and the roof. Double rows of razor-sharp teeth are open wide, and dread pools in my stomach. If they are here, does that mean the others are dead or badly injured somewhere behind them?

"Eric." Hunching down so I'm ready to intercept them, I throw a warning. "Incoming."

He is next to me before I'm finished talking, forgetting all about the troll tartar sauce he worked so hard to prepare. His horns circle his head like a crown that juts up for his temples. My breath hitches in my throat at how magnificent he looks with his glistening ebony skin and the wild hair tousled around his handsome face.

"Stop." This is no longer my Eric standing next to me. That voice, like rocks grinding while they slide over one another, belongs to Shadow—the Prince of Hell. "You must obey me."

The rogues freeze for a second, confused expressions marring their faces before they continue forward, inching this time. My mouth drops open, and I turn my glare on Eric.

"You have got to be shitting me." His head turns slightly my way and a line bunches up his forehead. "Are you serious right now?"

"I don't understand." His deep voice vibrates in my belly and chest.

Raphael grunts and huffs as he fights trolls behind us. I feel a dull ache sprouting from a couple of different places on my body, but it's nothing worrisome. No one has punched his light out, yet. How unfortunate.

"First, the two of you block me from fighting the trolls, and now you're sending them"—My finger stabs in the direction of the rogues—"away?"

If anything, the said rogues flinch back a few steps from my frustrated snarl.

Eric pins me with those otherworldly eyes of his, and his

penetrating gaze smacks me all the way in my soul. When he is in his human form, my mate is a growly pain in the ass who's too stubborn when it comes to my safety. Shifted into his true form, he is a predator, and mate or not, he recognizes strength more than anything else. Aware that this is a monumental moment and I will either screw it up or actually win the battle of wills, I stiffen my spine.

"I need to fight, Shadow." Calling him that feels strange, and I stutter, my tongue tripping on it. "I need to win. For me."

My skin feels too tight as he pulls the darkness around us, and like tendrils, he uses it to poke at me. Half of me wants to jump out of my body and run screaming, but the other part groans in delight and perks its head up. The dark side of who I am drinks in his shadows, and needs more, tugging at him to feed it. His gaze bores into me.

I don't dare look away.

The edges of his lips quirk.

This magnificent creature I call my mate gives me a barely there nod and steps away. My heart is hammering hard enough to bruise my ribcage, and I pant like I just ran a marathon. He turns to the rogues, giving them an unimpressed once over. "Fight."

My heart skips a beat.

The rogues chatter louder as they rush me, and I have no more time to think about what had just happened. With my dagger raised in front of me, I brace for the attack, my blood boiling from the adrenaline rushing through my veins.

"Playtime, motherfuckers." I pounce just as the first wave reaches me.

Eric's chuckle drowns their screams.

Chapter Fifteen

HELENA

Sweat trickles down my back as I slash, twist, turn, and bend in the hopes that I will avoid the sharp teeth and razor claws of our enemies from sinking into my skin. The odds are more evenly matched now that Eric is in his true form, although neither him nor Raphael have their wings out. And honestly, there is no way they'll fit in here like that.

Decapitated demons litter the ground around my feet, their numbers seeming to multiply with each kill I make. I'm starting to think there is a hole somewhere on the roof where they trickle in the tunnel like ants sensing something sweet, but I can't see anything past them to find out if my thought is right.

Eric and Raphael work in turns to take out the trolls. Unfortunately, the dumb creatures aren't as stupid as I'd originally believed because, instead of trying to bulldoze through the two males, they hold themselves back. They also switch out like tag-team wrestles when one gets tired or hurt too bad to continue. There are four hurt, but four others are left blocking that side of the tunnel.

"Are they coming from the roof?" Panting for breath that doesn't come, I kick a rogue soccer-ball style and call out to Eric. "Can you see?"

Raphael is right.

We should've brought Narsi. My sidekick would've eaten most of them by now.

"Only a dozen or so left." My mate grunts from the effort he puts into peppering punches on a troll, his voice coming at me through the soles of my feet.

"How"—I gasp to suck in air before I spin, using the momentum to high kick a rogue right in his ugly head—"nice."

The lowest class of demon shrieks like a banshee, running with his arms and legs flailing before he flies back like a cannon ball, taking a few of his buddies down with him. They turn on him with snapping jaws, and a horrified expression covers my face when I watch them eat half of his body. My dagger glows brighter while I fight the bile burning the back of my throat, though I can't pry my eyes from the sight for a too-long moment.

When I can finally look away, I realized Eric was right about one thing: there are not that many left. But I'm tired, sore, and thirsty as hell, so it still feels like there is a never-ending river of them coming at me. Not that I will stop or ask for help. I just gained a foothold with Eric's protective-ness, and I plan to fight until I can no longer lift a hand. Even after that, though, I'll use my teeth if need be. I think Narsi is rubbing off on me.

Choking on the acid flooding my mouth, I throw the dagger, embedding it in the middle of a rogue's forehead before jumping to snatch it and slice another's head almost completely off his shoulders. The ground quakes when another troll goes down, and it makes me stumble.

"The others." I don't dare say anything more. They are fine, I'm sure. They musgt not have heard the signal.

Grabbing a demon with my free hand, I yank as hard as I can, putting my back into it and flinging him at the wall. He smacks it like a melon dropped from a few stories high and slides down, leaving a dark smear on the concrete.

A demon screams from behind me, and I whirl around, strands of my hair slapping my face.

"I'm touched, she-devil. You were worried about us." Colt appears over the heads of the few rogues left, his smirk firmly in place.

My mouth twists at his arrogance, and I imagine it looks like I've taken a big bite of a rotten lemon. "Don't dilute yourself, Colt. I was worried about my father, Beelzebub, and George."

Said father popped out of nowhere behind Colt's shoulder, his eyes wide as they locked on me. "Do not worry, Helena. I will not perish while you need me."

My groan is wrenched from the bottom of my feet.

He misunderstands it, because of course he does.

"I give you my word, daughter. Do not fear." With plate-sized hands, he smacks the remaining rogues out of his way. One or two scramble away as if they are bolting for their lives.

I give Satanael my flattest look.

He grins proudly.

"Can you go help them with the trolls?" The question is not even out of my mouth yet when he puffs his chest and saunters to join Eric and Raphael.

"You okay?" George rushes to me, his hands fluttering around my arms. When he can't find a place not covered in black blood, he drops them to his sides.

"Yeah, it was just rogues." Even I can hear the petulance in my voice. "Apparently I'm not allowed to fight anything bigger than a Great Dane."

"You don't sound too happy about it." My hunter friend smiles so wide that his white teeth glint in the light still coming from Raphael.

"You think?" Beelzebub and Colt snicker at me, and I stick my tongue out at them.

Two more roars make me flinch, and I jerk my shoulders to my ears when the sound makes my brain rattle. The four of us turn in time to see my father, my mate, and my Archangel friend finish off the last troll. The poor thing doesn't have time to see where he is before his head is dangling on his shoulders, only attached by a thin piece of skin.

He goes down like timber, the ground quaking from the impact.

"It is done, Helena." Satanael turns with his puffed-out chest.

Why did I think it was a great idea to call him from Hell again?

Eric huffs a disgusted breath at my father and steps closer before shifting back to his normal self. His very naked, very aroused self, I might add. My eyes lock on his thick erection pointing accusingly at me and not my father. In that moment, they could bring my mother and half of my family line here, but there would still be no way I could tear my gaze away from it.

George nudges me with his shoulder.

"So,"—My gaze snaps to Eric's grinning face, and I clear my throat—"lots of creepy crawleys around here, huh?"

If they are still staring at me like they were before, I was going to slap myself across the forehead for sounding dumb.

"Only two trolls on the other side of the tunnel." Beelzebub takes pity on my miserable ass and changes the subject. "I think you stumbled on the gold mine."

My brain finally logs back online. "Which brings one question to the front of my mind: why?" They are looking at me like I have another head growing, so I frown at them. "As dumb as they are, I'm sure the trolls know they can barely fight in a tight place like this tunnel. Even without any common sense, their survival instincts alone will tell them that much."

"We are cleaning out the city," Raphael mumbles, baring his teeth while shaking his hands to clean the bloody particles sticking to his fingers. "It could've been the safest hole for them to hide in." He grunts a "thank you" when George pulls out a t-shirt from his backpack and hands it to him.

"You have a change of clothes in that thing?" The hunter just shrugs nonchalantly while avoiding my inquiring gaze. "I still think something feels off." Before they start with their macho displays, I rush to explain my perspective. "Yes, it could be the safest place they thought they could hide, but can they do wards?" One look around tells me no. "So maybe they were here because of the protection the jinn already had around it. Which bares the question: what did they find here? And is it still alive?"

"Down south is clear." Beelzebub rolls his shoulders like tension is weighing them down. "If there is anything left, it's up north."

"The trolls could've eaten it," Colt chirps, but he snaps his mouth shut when I scowl at him. "It is possible." Raising both hands in the air in front of him, he takes a few teetering steps back. "That's all I'm saying."

Satanael, who has thankfully kept his trap shut, closes his eyes and takes a lungful of air in through his nose. I expect him to tell us we are all idiots and beneath him before stepping away and back to Hell. Instead, his peepers snap open and lock on me. "There is something else in this tunnel." My breath hitches at the intensity of his stare. "It is not from Hell."

"My mother?" I have no idea why I think it'll be so easy to find her if she is indeed alive. Maybe because we found him in Atlanta so it makes me think she might be here too.

Satanael shakes his head, and a sorrowful look haunts his eyes. "It is too weak to be your mother's energy. An object perhaps? A lesser angel?" He glances at Raphael, who is resembling a statue while staring at my father.

"We shall find it." The Archangel nods sharply, throwing the blood-drenched t-shirt at his feet. "Whatever it is."

"Are you hurt, Hel?" Eric mumbles close to my ear, and I shiver from his nearness. He is naked, for fuck's sake, and my father is standing a couple of feet in front of us.

"Put pants on," I hiss at him, and the jerk chuckles. I wedge my elbow in his gut. The grunt that rips from him is music to my ears.

"Turn around so my mate can change her shirt," Eric barks at the rest of them, and they all snap around in some orchestrated, creepy dance. His backpack dangles between two fingers as he hands it to me.

With clenched teeth, I rummage through it and replace my blood-covered top. He finally covers his nakedness when I shove a pair of pants at his chest, too. Urgency churns inside me, but I'm too scared to hope. So, I say nothing until we are ready to move forward. Raphael once again repeats the same thing he said earlier as if reassuring himself.

"We will find it, whatever it is."

Or whoever it is, I thought to myself as I followed behind the rest of them with Eric by my side.

Chapter Sixteen

RAPHAEL

It is foolish to hope.

Not for the first time, I tell myself the same thing, yet I cannot help it. It prickles inside me, spreading faster than I can stop it. The blood sticks to my skin as a reminder that no matter how hard I try to do things right, someone has to pay dearly for it. Helena's words from not long ago haunt me even in my waking hours, her eyes glinting as she tilts her head up to lock them on me as if she could see to the core of my essence. *"You may be made of light, angel, but good you are not. Heaven's hands are washed in too much blood to be able to claim it just for themselves."* Her voice rings in my head like an accusation.

Darkness stretches in front of our progression, an open maw of a hungry beast that hides whatever heavenly light Satanael sensed not long ago. And here I am, a starving male pulled by its lure, my skin itching with the need to go near it so I can feel whatever little part of my home I can. Pathetic and utterly undeserved after the insanity overtaking my senses when I plunged myself in Purgatory to find Helena.

I didn't tell her what that means for me.

What it does to an Archangel.

Purgatory is the in-between of Heaven and Hell, the only place forbidden for both angels and demons alike. What Lucifer's son and I did against all odds cost both of us a lot. He doesn't show any indication that it has changed him, nor that he feels any different.

But I know.

I will never go home.

My feet will never grace the soil of Heaven, nor will I ever feel the warmth of my father's light against my skin. Bliss will no longer fill every particle of my being like an embrace so I know my part in these worlds. Now, I'll just drift like a tumbleweed for as long as I am needed. After that ...

In this moment of unbridled emotion, my eyes go to Helena.

Head bowed and forehead pinched, she stares at her feet while she walks. Clumps of hair crusted with demon blood sway around her shoulders, and her face is smudged with streaks of it like war paint. Whatever she couldn't clean off her skin only adds to the picture she presents. One glance around the others, and it's clear as day.

I'm not the only one changed because of the female. Nor is Eric unchanged for trespassing Purgatory with me. We have all altered our very essence because of her. And that is when it hits me like a blow to the chest, stealing my breath away. I will no longer see my home, but not for reasons I want to give myself to feed my guilt.

Helena *is* home.

For me. For Lucifer's son, for Satanael, and for the rest of our unlikely party.

What does it all mean?

"I do not think Shadow will appreciate it much if you keep ogling my daughter," Satanael throws at me conversationally, though he doesn't take his eyes off the tunnel.

I balk from the offhanded comment. "I do not ogle anyone." The twitch of his mouth says he hears the defensive tone in my voice. "I do not," I add firmly.

"If that is what you wish to tell yourself, very well. You do not." He falls silent after a slow nod of his head.

I glower at the pitch-black space before us. *I do not ogle Helena,* I state firmly in my head, nodding as well like that will confirm it—as if it will make his accusation go away.

"Does she know how you feel?" Satanael speaks low enough for our ears only, but that doesn't stop me from rubbernecking to check over my shoulder to make sure the rest of them are far away from this preposterous conversation. "I suppose not."

"She is Zadkiel's daughter." My snarl makes him grin like a fool. "That is what I feel. Now watch ahead and lead us to whatever you sense in this God-forsaken hole."

"Whatever you say, Archangel." When I side-eye him, I see his chest rocking with silent chuckling.

My fists clench at my sides.

"Do you feel it, Raphael?" Eric calls from behind me, and panic short-circuits my senses.

Whirling around, I rush him and point my finger at his face. "I do not feel anything." Everyone freezes at my feral hiss. "Nothing." I punctuate it by stabbing the air once more, my fingertip an inch from his nose.

Satanael chuckles.

"If you don't remove your finger from my face, I will rip it off and shove it so far up your nose you'll be able to scratch your shriveled brain with it." Eric's jaw is set, and he glares at me.

Understanding dawns that he hasn't heard what Satanael and I said. He is asking if I can sense the light we are searching for, and not anything about what I feel or don't feel for his mate. Heat spreads from my neck up to my face, festering around my cheekbones. Dropping my hand, I square my shoulders, tugging on my crusted shirt to straighten it primly.

"My apologies." If Satanael does not stop snickering, I will punch his lights out. "I was focused on it and reacted in a way that was uncalled for. We are not near it yet."

"Can we do dick-measuring contests later?" Helena shoulders her way between us, pressing a hand on both of our chests. "My legs hurt, and I want to sit down for a moment." Leaning to the side, she blinks at her father. "Is that okay? We can rest for like ten minutes?"

"We will rest twenty minutes, daughter," the prick gloats, throwing pointed glances to the side of my head. "We can all use it, it seems. All this tension will do us no good."

Maybe I can knock him out. I bet no one will hold it against me.

"You two are coming with me." Helena narrows her eyes on Eric and me before tugging us along with her to the side of the tunnel. After she lowers herself on the ground, she points to either side of her. "Sit. I don't trust that you won't bicker like old maids if I don't keep an eye on you. I have a headache."

I stiffen.

Eric joins her, not taking his glare off my face while I shuffle my feet like a youngling, uncomfortable and wary.

Leave it to Satanael to get inside my head and fill it with nonsense. He doesn't understand anything about me. About Zadkiel. Why do I care what he thinks, anyway? It is none of his concern what goes through my head, or my heart for that matter.

As soon as I fold myself next to Helena, she sighs and rests her head on my shoulder, one of her hands stretching out to hold Eric's. My heart thumps hard against my ribcage, stuttering there for a long moment before splattering at my feet.

"Is it just me, or does this seem wrong somehow to you, too?" Helena mutters to no one in particular. The others spread through the tunnel, stretching out and talking among themselves.

"It is wrong." It comes out harsher than I intended.

She tilts her head to peer up at my face. "Right? It feels off somehow like we aren't seeing the whole picture, and we are going headfirst into a trap."

Oh.

We are still talking about whatever Satanael sensed and not his asinine accusations.

Right.

Eric leans forward to spear me with a look over his mate. "What in Hell's name is the matter with you anyway, Angel?" A mocking curl of his lips brings a glint in his eye. "Did the trolls knock on your skull a few too many times?"

"Maybe that's why I have a headache." Helena joins in on his joke, her soft giggle warming me inside.

The tension tightening my body loosens, and I press my back harder on the wall behind me. Joining in, I nudge her gently with my shoulder, chuckling as well at Eric's jab. "I will let a troll knock me around any day as long as Satanael stays away from me with his incoherent chattering. All it does is mess with my mind."

And that is how, as humans would say, I put my foot in my mouth.

"What did he say?" Helena perks up straight away.

I mush my lips together with a groan.

"Raphael," she says my name as a warning and pokes me in the stomach.

Teeth clenched, I tilt my head back and close my eyes. "He likes to tell me how I feel or don't feel. It is not of importance, Helena. Do not worry."

"That's where you are wrong, mister. I do worry." She rounds on her mate. "Eric, tell him to start talking before we get stuck here for days. I'm not moving until he tells me what's going on. Or until I beat it out of him."

Cracking my eyelids open, I smile at her frown. "Maybe I deserve a good beating once in a while."

"You act like you've never met Hel," Eric grumbles from her other side. "Just tell her what she wants to know, and I might catch a two-minute nap." He grunts when she elbows him. "You told me to make him talk."

My laugh bubbles out and echoes around us.

I will not tell her the truth regardless.

Not all of it, at least.

"After Purgatory, I may never step back in Heaven." She sucks in a breath that speaks volumes about the gravity of my revelation.

"Oh, Raphael." Sorrow saturates her tone, and she hugs me so tightly my ribs protest from it. "We will figure it out, I promise. There must be a way. There must be." Her voice is muffled from my shirt.

"I am sure if anyone can find a resolution, it'll be you, Helena." My eyes lock on Eric's over her head.

He stares at me unblinking as he tries to read what I did not say. My heartbeat speeds up for a moment, and my arm wraps around her shoulders, but I don't look away. Satanael's words swirl in my head like a cloud of bees, but that's nonsense. I would be at peace if another, very distant voice didn't rear its head in the furthest corners of my mind.

What if Satanael speaks the truth?

Chapter Seventeen

HELENA

My heart hurts for Raphael.

From day one, when I felt lost, alone, and forgotten in that cursed white room where my blood was used daily like I was a human-sized Capri-sun by the jinn pretending to be Michael, this Archangel was my light in the darkness. His presence gave me hope that help was coming. That I wouldn't be locked away forever until Death decided to lead me away. Raphael talked to me, healed me, and just knowing I would see his angelic face from time to time made me stronger when I had no strength left.

While his presence represented better things coming for me, I had doomed him for all eternity.

How's that for a punch in the gut?

"Maybe you should walk with us." I tug on Raphael's sleeve when he tries to move ahead of me and Eric. "No one needs to suffer my father's arrogance unless it's the last option left."

We ended up resting for a couple of hours, collapsing around the tunnel instead of in my requested ten minutes

The fight shouldn't have tired us that much, or me, I should say, but with all the changes in my body, my limbs are sometimes too heavy to move.

My tail flicks behind me, and my butt clenches.

"Very well," Raphael agrees reluctantly, his golden eyes locked on my hand where I am scratching at my small horns.

I drop my hand sheepishly. "I'm still not used to them." Leave it to me to share unnecessary information.

"You make them look good." Raphael smiles, and Eric grunts an agreement. "They suit you."

"Because I charge like a raging bull all the time?" ?y snickering is filled with unease. "I can see the need for them when put like that." A squeal is torn from me when Eric wraps his fingers around my tail.

Hips jerking forward, I dart ahead and tug as hard as I can to remove my wiggling appendage from his grasp. Both of them throw their heads back at the same time, one light and golden, the other mysterious and dark, roaring their laughter at the roof. Like a dumbass, I gape at them open-mouthed, my throat tightening with emotions. The others chuckle and snort from ahead of us, but I don't pay them any attention. Especially since my father has been darting glances loaded with meaning at the three of us.

I swallow thickly.

"Laugh it off." Grumbling under my breath, I yank my tail out of Eric's hand. "Jerks."

"But you are so beautiful when you are angry, Hel." Eric grins at me, and Raphael nods. "I can almost see the smoke coming out of your ears."

"If I stick the pointy bit of my dagger in your eyeballs, you won't see jack shit." My smile oozes sweetness. "Wanna try?"

"Just kidding, cupcake." Both hands up and palms in the air, he takes a step back. "Let's not resort to stabbing. I'm sure we will come across something in this tunnel that will warrant your blade, an eyeball, or maybe something even better."

"Can you imagine how you'll feel if you start glowing the same way Raphael does?" I ask my mate, and he shudders with revulsion. "See? Not so funny now, is it?" My pointed finger turns to the Archangel. "How about you growing a tail, huh? A rope wiggling over your ass day and night." Judging by the expression twisting his angelic features, I'd say Raphael is horrified. "Right. So let's not make fun of Helena while she deals with all that shit, okay?"

And now I've started referring to myself in third person.

Lovely.

When I stumble a step, anger bubbles inside me for a second because I think my frustration with them laughing at me makes me trip. George gasping whips my head up, though, and I see everyone springing their arms to the sides to keep their balance. Another shudder under our feet has us all pitching sideways, my hipbone smarting like a mother when I lean over the metal track. I can hear the bone smacking over the hard surface, and bright dots bloom in my vision. A few more shudders rock me where I'm stretched on the floor before silence falls over us.

Dust and debris rain over us all.

I lift my head, flipping hair off my face in time to see everyone is on the ground like me, apart from Raphael. The Archangel looms above us with his arms extended wide to the sides, and he points a narrowed glare at the roof of the tunnel. I follow his line of sight, and my heart skips a beat when I see cracks spiderwebbing through every visible surface. Scrambling to my feet, I join him, not taking my eyes off it.

"Is it going to cave in?" A tremor rakes my spine.

"It'll hold," he murmurs, still eyeing it strangely. "For now."

"It could've been like that before we entered the tunnels," Colt, ever the helpful, chirps while dusting his pants.

"I will not test the validity of your words with my mate's life," Eric drawls at his twin from Raphael's other side. The fact that his ass was lying on the ground the same way mine was when the earthquake—or whatever it was—rocked the earth soothed my pride.

My fingers brush the hilt of the dagger strapped to my thigh.

We've been in this tunnel for hours now. I have no doubt it's bright daylight outside, and I know deep down that I won't breathe the smoke-filled air of Atlanta anytime soon. So far, only one terminal is left behind us, and a lot more are waiting ahead. Everything in me screams that we should go back to the safe house and resume our search tomorrow, but my lips are glued shut. Going back and forth will only waste more time and we were ready to go on this trip anyway, even before we decided to start by combing MARTA first.

"The human realm has made you all weak," Satanael snarls at the rest of them, his face turning a darker shade of burgundy. The pointed tip of his tail snaps in agitation behind him.

"I've always been here, man." George frowns at my father, taking offense on behalf of everyone else. It's fun to see my hunter friend sticking his neck out for Hell's creatures, as he liked to call them until not long ago. "I'm actually stronger with them around, not weaker."

"You know you're talking to Satan, right George?" I can't stop the grin from stretching my lips when he pales and gulps. "Sorry, I had to say it out loud." Eric snorts at my giggles, smirking at the hunter.

Satanael bares his teeth at me, but it looks like he's attempting to smile.

I'm not sure, though.

"Anyway, let's keep moving before another wave rocks this tunnel and drops it on our heads." Shivering, I take the first step. "I really don't want to be buried alive here."

"The human is right." Beelzebub, speaking for the first time in a while, glances at my father. That's one thing I like about him. He never feels the need to fill the silence with useless words. When he does say something, however, I've noticed everyone pays attention.

Including Satanael.

"Should the human take your place in Hell, then?" Leave it to my father to find any way he can to insult people. And he does it without even trying, I swear. He's natural at it.

"Perhaps, although I do believe he is more needed here." Beelzebub doesn't take the bait.

Good for him.

With a grunt, Satanael stomps forward, his lips pursed like he is sucking on a lemon. I shuffle behind, dragging my tired legs and rubbing my sore hipbone like a masochist. Each press of my fingers numbs my whole side to the juncture where my thigh is attached to my pelvis. Meanwhile, I observe Satanael.

Somehow I missed how tense his shoulders are, and how his spine is ramrod straight. His fists keep clenching and unclenching at his sides, too—a fact that doesn't go unnoticed now that I'm focused on him He doesn't walk ahead of me, either. No, he is prowling like a predator who just caught the scent of his prey and is following it with single-minded focus. But it's not just the search that has him stiff like he has a stick up his ass. My father is arrogance personified on the best of days, but the way he holds himself, there is more to it than that. It hits me like a rock over my head.

My stomach drops to my feet.

Satanael is hiding something.

Chapter Eighteen

ERIC

Unease rides my ass, but I do my best not to show it in front of Helena. No one can convince me that the concrete walls cracking and encasing us inside this tunnel is from natural causes. My mate mentioned it when we stopped to rest, and I agreed with her words.

Something feels off.

The terminal chases out the darkness, its flickering lights piercing the shadows and sending them away. Helena speeds toward it like a moth lured by a flame, and I stay in step with her. Raphael glides faster, too, his shoulders swinging and full of determination. Satanael messed with the poor pricks head earlier, and although he is back to his old self, I see him glancing sideways at my mate like he expects her to do something.

Or like he is afraid of her.

But that's preposterous.

"We can take the stairs to the top at this terminal and follow the trail above ground." Satanael turns his head at my comment. "Unless you have to turn into a mole to sense whatever we are in search of?" His glower is my reward.

I grin at him.

Satanael flicks his eyes at his daughter, thinks better of whatever is going through his head, and keeps his mouth shut. I'll be damned. The King of Wrath is picking his battles. Maybe Hell will freeze over soon, an expression I've heard many humans say.

"Actually, I'd rather we continue through the tunnel." Helena looks from me to Raphael. "I don't want to miss any creatures that might still lurk here and can corner us when we eventually have to come back down. Unless you think the roof might not hold."

Since no one says otherwise, we pass the brightly lit station with a single glance and plunge back into darkness, trotting over the rail tracks. Hiking the strap of my backpack higher on my shoulder, I reach for Helena's hand, lacing our fingers together. She gives me a thin smile but offers a reassuring squeeze.

"At least we are not the only dumbasses who have walked here." She points at the far right wall and the scribbled graffiti on it.

The faded paint swirls into elaborate circles that overlap one another with a few sharp jutted points at the edges. Absently, I trace them with my eyes as we move by them, my neck straining as I attempt to keep them in sight long after.

"They are not that interesting," Hel grumbles under her breath, and I drag my gaze away from the scribbles.

"It made me think—" I start, but as always, Colt has to interject his stupidity into everything.

"That's the problem." His fingers snap with a dull echo.

"I wondered what your problem was, but there you have it. You were actually thinking."

Raphael snorts but sobers fast when I stare at him flatly.

"As I was saying before I was rudely interrupted." Casting a cursory glance at the narrow path and low railing on both sides, I zero in on Satanael's furrowed brow. "Some of these doors must open despite the chains and locks on them. Whoever painted that, I'm sure they didn't waltz through the security of the metro station without blinking an eye."

"Why do you say that?" Beelzebub, always the one wanting to be prepared for anything, slides closer to the railing. "It could've been painted after the attacks on the city. We haven't found all the humans hiding like rats all over."

"That was painted long before the attack. It's too faded."

"What are you thinking, Shadow?" Satanael growls when Colt snorts at his question.

I ignore my twin.

"Since we came across the trolls and rogues, I kept asking myself how they managed to come at us from both sides when neither of us heard or sensed anything." Removing my fingers from Helena, I press my palm on her lower back to guide her one step ahead of me. "It looked too organized to be accidental."

"You're trying to say they knew we were going to be in that exact spot and popped in the tunnel on purpose?" The horror on my mate's face doesn't sit well with me, but we have to look at all angles.

Raphael steps closer to her, and she instantly calms.

A frown pinches my forehead at that.

Shaking my head, I turn to Satanael again. "All I'm

saying is if some of these doors do open, we need to proceed with caution. No more surprises."

With a nod, he starts swiveling his head once so often, checking every discoloration on the walls we pass like it's an enemy he needs to install fear into. Colt, for all his pestering, pays closer attention to our surroundings, following on Beelzebub's footsteps in case the other male fails to see a huge door embedded in the concrete.

"It could've been them in this part of the tunnel instead of us." Raphael voices my turbulent thoughts. "Helena was not the target if it was indeed an attack."

I'm not so sure about that.

"You guys are incorrigible." The attempt to lighten the mood falls flat with Helena's worried tone. "Not everyone is out to get me, you know. I'm pretty sure some of these idiots are just happy to be out of Hell."

"I can relate to that." She flashes me a smile when I mumble my agreement with her, but it rings in my own ears.

"You would, wouldn't you?" My twin jabs from the side, unaware that hurt is plastered all over his face. I doubt he will ever forgive me for leaving him behind when I walked out on my father.

My mouth opens, ready to say … something. Apologize maybe?

I never get the chance.

"Do you hear that?" Satanael jerks to a stop, his hand lifting next to his head into the universal sign to hold.

We all freeze in the spot.

I hold my breath, not daring to make a sound as I strain my ears, but I don't hear anything. The backpack slides down my arm, and I drop it with a dull thud before tugging Helena to my chest. Keeping her there with one arm around her waist, I cock my head as if that will somehow help reveal whatever sounds Satanael is listening to in his head. When Raphael turns his back and moves closer to sandwich my mate between us, my tense muscles uncoil.

Shadows dance over everyone's faces from the glow emanating from Raphael, forming sharp angles on their cheekbones and jawlines. Deeper in the darkness from where the three of us are clustered, their eyes, apart from the human, glow like a cat's when faced with a flashlight. Dread pools in my gut, weighing me down.

That's when I feel it.

Leave it to Satanael to confuse the senses. It's not a sound that got his attention at all. It's a sensation that I wish I never felt, but there is nothing I can do. I have to get Helena out of here, now.

The ground under our feet vibrates.

At first, it's a gentle brush under the soles of my boots, but the longer I'm focused on it, the stronger it gets. I physically see it the moment the rest of them realize what is going on. One by one, they stiffen, their heads whipping around to gawk at the others. Urgency kicks me in the ass, and I tighten my arm around Helena.

She gasps.

From how hard I grab her or from noticing the vibrations, I'm not sure, and I don't care. Lifting her off the ground, I throw her over my shoulder and spin for the side of the tunnel, where I can see a deeper shadow indicating there is a door there. Locked or unlocked, I'll rip it with my hands if I have to, but we are getting out of here.

"There." My shout booms in the silence a moment later, and it's followed by an insistent buzzing. It builds in my ears like pressure threatening to blow my eardrums to shreds.

Keeping my arm raised and finger pointed, I sprint for it with everything in me. "Move."

Thudding footsteps follow my lead as we bolt for what I think is a damn door. It better be because we are too large to fit in the narrow path and stay unharmed. It was made for humans, not beasts of our size to use as a safe passage. We will be swept away and shredded to a bloody pulp in seconds unless we get out of the cemented death trap we willingly entered.

A shrill horn splits the air, turning my blood to ice.

The train is coming.

Chapter Nineteen

HELENA

My brain still can't register what's happening.

One second, Eric is trying to tell us something while his brother pokes jokes at him, and the next, we are all standing like statues spread around the tracks in some twisted circle, wide-eyed and terrified. My stomach protests when Eric's shoulder lodges itself in my gut, and I clench my teeth so I don't yell at him to put me down. My hair sways across his ass and thighs, and I grunt like a pig when it starts running.

Unable to get enough air in my lungs, I clutch his lower back, grinding my teeth. Thank fuck I'm doing that because when the horn of a train screams in my ears, I would've bitten my tongue. Horror numbs me, a bone-deep chill that not even Raphael's hand splayed between my shoulders can thaw.

"George." Lifting my head as much I can, I shriek for my friend. He is not as fast as the rest of them, and there is no way I'll keep my mouth shut and let them leave him behind. "George." The desperation in my screams raises goosebumps all over my skin.

"Colt has the human," Raphael huffs, practically shoving us in front of him.

The tunnel is deafening from the thundering of the incoming train.

Eric dumps me on my feet out of nowhere, and I flail my arms so I don't flop on my back. I didn't need to worry because my tailbone smacks the railing hard enough to bend my tail into a horrible angle, eliciting another squeal. The pain makes me run in place like I need to pee, but it's either that or start crying like an idiot in front of everyone.

My heart is thudding in sync with the oncoming monstrosity that is about to turn all of us into pancakes.

My mate wraps his large hand around the chain on the doorknob and yanks on it with everything in him. The metal links groan and snap, tinkling as they hit the ground around his feet, but the door doesn't budge. All of us crowd around him, so close that I'm pretty sure I just shoved my boob into Satanael's upper arm. The more I prance in one spot, the more hands brush against different parts of my body. Beelzebub almost trips over the railing when, in my attempt to avoid boobing my father again, I poke my ass into his groin.

"Sorry." My murmured apology passes through numb, frozen-solid, lips. The place where the tail grows from my body hurts like a bitch still.

My teeth are chattering.

Eric's hand slips off the brass knob a couple of times, though he continues to desperately try to open it. Sincde that isn't working, he pulls his arm back, missing my face by an inch as he smashes his fist on the metal plate around it. The wall around us vibrates, but I'm pretty sure that's from the freaking train and not the punch.

"No more than thirty seconds." As cool as a cucumber, my father announces the time like a damn conductor.

Trembling in my boots, I will Eric's hand to split the metal so he can wrench the door open. The metal chain and the lock keep clinking when he shuffles his feet to get a better stance, then he puts more power behind the hammering he is doing on it. Cold sweat trickles down my spine, not for myself, though. If worse comes to worst, I can plaster my back on the wall, close my eyes, and wait it out. Even George will fit, which he showcases by hugging the wall, and I imagine his lips are moving in prayers.

The others, however ...

None of them will survive.

Grunting and snarling sounds fade with the thundering of the incoming train. I latch onto Raphael's hand, squeezing his fingers like that will somehow open the cursed door because, no matter what Eric does to it, it doesn't budge. I bump into the Archangel when Colt shoulders behind him and takes Eric's place. Shivering in Raphael's arms, I watch him unblinking when he steps back and rams his shoulder at the slab of metal.

What is this damn thing made of?

The image of a tight, low tunnel on the other side of it, or maybe even stairs, mocks me in my mind's eye. The twins take turns, driving into it together when one proves not enough.

"Fifteen seconds." My father, the conductor, chirps, and I can't help it.

I kick at him, the tip of my boot connecting with his shin.

He shrugs.

"You'll be the first to be pulverized under the tracks." My voice is cracking, but I don't give a shit. "I'll push you before it takes any of the others, especially if you don't stop telling me the time of impact."

"Hel." My anger at Satanael forgotten, I lift my gaze to Raphael. Very rarely he calls me anything but Helena, so it comes as a shock. "Step aside."

Scrambling back to give him space, I don't waste time. Instead, I do what he asks. My heart in my throat, I watch as he joins the twins, but not even his added strength helps. Now that my hands are pressed close to the door, my pinky almost brushing the frame, I feel it. My hammering organ drops from my throat to my feet.

"Wards." It comes out as a whisper that they shouldn't be able to hear, but they do. "It's warded."

Satanael wraps his hand over Beelzebub's shoulder and nods. The other male latches onto Eric and so on until Colt grabs hold of Raphael. Power blooms around us, while tendons on their necks tighten, more visible because of the light coming from the train.

It'll pass us in less than ten seconds.

The door opens.

The twins step inside and roar in fury.

"It's a maintenance closet," Eric snarls.

I don't waste time because we have none left. "You get inside. Hurry. George and I will be okay." My hunter friend nods and squeezes his eyes shut again.

Eric protests, threatening everyone to get them to move out of his way, but luckily, they trust me more than he does. Asshole. Beelzebub and Satanael squeeze inside, too, and I shove Raphael's back to get him to move faster. At the added resistance, I poke my head around him, and I want to die the same instant. My father's back is peeking out of the door.

There is no room for the Archangel.

Tears drip over my cheeks, burning a trail across my cold skin. My hair whips around my face when Raphael flips, pressing me on the wall with his chest. The train shrieks around the corner, creating a vacuum of cold air that swirls around us, and there is nothing I can do to stop what's about to happen.

My face tilts up, and my eyes lock on the warm glow of the Archangel's golden one's.

There are so many emotions there that they still whatever air I have left in my lungs. Till the last moment, he stands in front of me to protect me with his body, as well as his life.

Ducking his head, Raphael presses his warm, soft lips on my forehead.

Then he is gone.

Ripped from me forever.

Chapter Twenty

HELENA

Rage.

All I feel is rage, and it drowns out everything. The fear, heartache, and sorrow all evaporates the way the shrieking wind blasting around me dries my tears. My scream is ripped from the very center of my soul, and it rises higher than the thundering of the passing train. In the reflection of the streaking windows, a stranger has her mouth open on a silent shout.

Her blonde hair dances around her head with flames flickering at the tips, and the red horns match the fire perfectly. A golden glow transforms her skin and makes it translucent, and the same flames, only a deeper red, swirl under it like a living thing. Her green eyes are lit like lanterns, wide and lost. It's in a split second that I see her, and a new wave of rage blasts through me.

I have no idea what I'm doing when my fingers brush against Satanael's back, and his head tilts back just enough for him to see me from the corner of his eye. My chin jerks at the still passing train, and my father gives me a sharp nod.

With one deep breath, I bend my knees and jump.

With one arm outstretched, I latch onto the protruding metal on the side of the train, my body crushing to it so harshly my grunt is lost in the shrieking wind around my ears. Brain numbing pain spreads over my shoulder, the damn thing nearly ripping my arm off when I plaster myself on it. A second after my body smacked it like a bug splattering a windshield, I feel another thump behind me, this one much stronger than my weight smacking on the metal. A few more follow.

Fingers aching, I claw my way to the top of the train, refusing to think that Raphael is dead or about what Eric will say about me throwing myself at the moving monstrosity the way I did. All my limbs shake from the effort when I sprawl on my back on the roof, panting and gasping. Raising only my head, I look down my body to find Satanael hugging the train with a feral grin on his face.

Darting my gaze over his bulky shoulders, I see Beelzebub's snarl and his bright, feverish red eyes. He nods when he sees me watching him. I guess the three of us are going to play Indiana Johns. I'll deal with Eric later after I make sure that … what? That Raphael is dead?

I refuse to think about anything right now.

Flipping on my belly, I start snaking up the length of the train. Hand over hand, my boots scrape the metal as I push myself toward the front. It felt like a couple of seconds between the Archangel being snatched away and me jumping, but I have more than half of the train length to crawl to reach my destination. My father and Beelzebub keep pace, and Satanael's head bumps the sole of my boot a few times.

With all the noise, there's no way for me to ask if they

saw what happened. Did the front of the train catch Raphael and pull him in, or was it the side? No matter what, I have to see for myself. Or maybe I just couldn't stay back and see pieces of his body and puddles of his blood left in the wake of the cursed train.

Occasionally, I pause and stick my head to the side, eyeing the length to check for anything. A blurred ground and wall meets my eyes, but that is it. Tears burn the back of my eyes, but I refuse to let them fall. I will not cry for him until the last moment, until I know without a shadow of a doubt that he is gone.

He can't be gone.

I cling to that with all I have.

My progress is slow. Much slower than I like, but I keep going. The others follow behind me, and I promise myself that when this is over, I will give Satanael the biggest hug of his very long life for having my back, no matter how foolish I'm being. Bright lights blind me twice as the train zips through two stations, and I still haven't reached the front.

Raphael's parting gaze looms in the back of my mind like an added weight, pressing me to the roof of the train and making me sluggish. My nails break while I claw my way forward, but I'll reach my destination if it's the last thing I do. Lost in my head, it takes me a second to realize I'm no longer sliding because a hand is holding my ankle.

Lifting my face off the metal, I look down the length of my body at Satanael. A jolt passes through my inside at his animated face, and I watch dumbly as he points to the side of the train repeatedly. Shit scared to look but wanting to see with all I am, I take hold of the edge and drag myself to the side.

There is nothing but the blurred line of the ground.

My glare will melt Satanael's face if it's possible, but my

father only shakes his head and stabs his finger at the side of the train again. Grinding my teeth, I peer over the edge one more time, avoiding looking all the way down. The useless hope that spears me dwindles the longer I stare with nothing to show for it. It's just a fucking train. Metal slabs put together, stupid wheels casting sparks occasionally, a line of freaking windows with one of them broken, and nothing else. No …

Wait, what?

I almost drop off the roof when I yank myself closer to look at the shattered window. My hair slaps my face, and I rip it aside with enough force to make my scalp tingle. With my heart in my throat, I stare frozen at the carriage where shards are sprinkled on the floor, and between two rows of fabric-adorned seats, a boot sticks out like a beacon. My happiness turns to terror when I take note of all the blood there, and around the jagged pieces sticking out like the hungry jaw of a shark from the broken window.

My head whips back to show Satanael that we might've found the Archangel, and the forced smile freezes on my face. Now that I'm almost dangling on the side of the cursed train, I see three more bodies lined up behind Beelzebub. George jumped, too? The tears that have been threatening to fall trickle down my cheeks.

Satanael taps on my foot, probably wondering what we are doing. Mind spinning with one idea after another, I stare at him because none of them seem possible. I'm small enough to slide down and hopefully jump through the hole where the window was busted open, but none of them can follow. Well, maybe George, but I'd rather not test that theory. The train doesn't look like it's planning to stop anytime soon either, and if this was deliberately done like Eric suggested, it'll continue until we hit something at the end and explode, dying in flames of glory for all I know.

No, we have to jump off, but not without Raphael. *If that is Raphael, girl, IF,* a dumb voice drawls, but I shove it away.

Mind made up, I wiggle around until my head is facing Satanael's. Shuffling closer until my mouth is level with his ear, I yell from the top of my lungs. "We need to jump off before it reaches the end of the rail tracks. It's not stopping." Unnecessarily, I explain something so obvious. I mean, there is not a soul inside that train. "I'm going to slide inside through the broken window before we pass the next station. If that's Raphael, I will push him out first." I have absolutely no idea how I'm going to lift and throw the Archangel. "If I don't have time to jump, I'll wait until the next one. Meet me there?"

Pulling back, I lock gazes with him.

My father searches my face, his jaw set. I can see all the arguments he wants to throw my way because they flicker through his irises fast enough to make me feel dizzy. Since I have no clue how much longer we have to go before the big bang, I nod once and start turning away from him. He will listen or not, and there is nothing I can do about it now. Fingers crossed, he will at least tell the others.

I agreed to this insanity and searching in the hopes we'd find my mother. As pathetic as that sounds. I never agreed to lose anyone in the process, and I'll be damned if I tuck tail—literally—and sulk without fighting to the last moment for any of them. The Fates gave not just Eric but Raphael to me as well. Resembling a spider, I spin until facing forward, pausing yet again.

Shouldn't I have felt it if the train killed the Archangel?

There is a hollow void in my chest, yes, but that may just

be from the thought of never seeing him again. My body hurts in places I never knew existed, but that can be explained since I jumped on a moving fucking train. Shaking my head, I push that aside, too.

I'm just wasting time.

Swallowing thickly, I don't give myself time to overthink things. As soon as I'm level with the broken window, I swing my legs to the side and slide down the body of the train until the tips of my boots catch the sill of the shattered glass. Muscles twitching and frozen, I take a deep breath and jerk as hard as I can forward with my hips, almost bending backwards before toppling inside the empty carriage.

A ferocious roar echoes from the outside, rattling the still standing windows.

My head pops up, and I lock my eyes on golden ones that are way too muted for my liking. Eric can be pissed all he wants.

I found Raphael, and he is alive.

For now.

Chapter Twenty-One

ERIC

I'm going to kill her.

Me. I will personally wrap my fingers around her neck and twist until I pop the sense back into her head. My chest still aches for the Archangel, too. Besides how much he means to her, I came to terms with having him around all the time. I don't like it, but ...

I tolerate it for her sake.

Be that as it may, I'm not willing to place Helena's life on the line for anyone, east of all for the Archangel. But does she care what I think?

Of course not.

"She will get Raphael and push him off on the next station. She's the only one that can fit. We jump." Beelzebub roars in my ear, and I glare at him. Like fuck I'm jumping anywhere while my mate is inside a metal contraption headed for destruction. "Tell the others." With that, he flops around and edges to the side, preparing for it.

Jaw clenched hard enough my molars hurt, I turn to tell my twin to jump, and my eyebrows crawl to my hairline when the human scrambles on top of Colt to hear what I have to say. Repeating what Beelzebub told me, I have no energy to jab at my brother about the situation. His comment stops me, however.

"You are not jumping." It's a statement, not a question, so I hold his gaze. "I'll stay, too."

"Me too," the human yells, as well, with a stubborn tilt to his chin, though the wind swallows his voice.

I like him.

Colt sucks in a sharp breath, and I jerk my head over my shoulder just in time to see Helena swing her legs off the train. Terror I've never known clamps my chest and squeezes until I fully expect my ribcage to burst. It was not enough to die inside when the speed train carried her away while I pretended to be a sardine in a maintenance closet, but now she wants me to watch her do suicidal stunts a second time and not do anything about it.

Dragging myself to the edge, I peer down at the space between the moving contraption and the railing, cursing up a storm when I confirm there is no way for me to dangle like her without having half of my body shredded in half.

"You won't fit," Colt shouts from behind me, his arm clamping over my legs as he pulls himself closer. I think he is learning tricks from the human.

"No shit," I spit out in anger.

Helena's hair flings up in the air, writhing like standing snakes before her flingers disappear from the edge, and then she is gone. My twin's hold on me is the only thing keeping me on top of the train when I surge forward to join her.

"I can go." George is now on top of my legs. Since when did they start using me as a mattress?

Kicking them both off me but mindful not to shove them off the cursed thing, I pull myself forward, passing

Beelzebub with only a few grunts from him. Satanael is a problem, however, so I glance around to see how to maneuver around his large frame. Without my groin getting close and personal with his ass, that is.

He cranes his neck and pins me with a glare. "Do not even think about it."

"I'm going down there." By my estimation, we should be almost on top of the next station. Time is of the essence.

Wind whips around my head, and the longer strands of my hair stab my eyes. It takes everything in me not to kick them all off this damn thing and go after my mate. What is it that they don't understand? The more time we spend engaged in this staring match, the longer she is alone dealing with who knows what.

Is Raphael even alive?

"It is her choice, Shadow." Satanael picks the worst fucking time to lecture me on relationships. "You must trust her."

"Like you trusted Zadkiel?" My sneer is uncalled for, but I can't find it in me to care. "How did that end up for you?"

A muscle twitches under his left eye.

"I need to get down." Maybe if I say it a few times, he will make space for me to crawl closer.

"No." The prick even spreads his legs, so now I can't even edge around him.

Fuck.

Dizziness overtakes me, and I drop my forehead on the cold metal, closing my eyes. Nostrils flaring, I take deep breath after deep breath, hoping I don't toss my cookies all over both of us. Well, all of us actually, with the wind streaking down the length of the train. Emotions flood me —helplessness, fear, regret …

It should've never come to this.

After Purgatory and all that bullshit, Helena should be safe. We need to rebuild whatever is left of the city and take a breather, for fuck's sake, not repeat what went on before I had to kill my mate. Try as I may, I will never be able to erase or escape that memory. It'll haunt me for as long as I live, even with Helena by my side. And her own father wants me to stand back and watch her plunge into the first danger that comes her way.

No can do.

"She knows what she is doing," Beelzebub growls from behind me, but he doesn't help.

Propping myself on my elbows, I glance down at him. "Does she? She saw Raphael die for her. Plus … it's Helena."

Beelzebub grins, and he can't hide the affection he has for her from me.

"Is he alive?" I hear myself ask, and I clamp my mouth shut.

"Yes," Satanael answers, proving he pays too close attention for someone who trusts his daughter's decisions. "He must be." His mutter is for himself, but the wind carries his words to my ears regardless.

"Let me pass, Satanael." My throat is raw from shouting.

"And have her mad at me because you want to kill yourself to prove a point?" One of his eyebrows arches, and it's so much like Helena that I can't breathe. "No."

I wouldc already be down there with her by now if these assholes would stop being more stubborn than mules. The scraping of my teeth as I grind them together makes me shiver, but no matter what I say or do, there is no getting around Satanael. I'll have to wait like an idiot until he jumps so I can line up with the broken window I saw him pointing at before my mate made the crazy decision to go through it.

"Station." Beelzebub jerks a hand, pointing at the bright light peaking from around the corner.

This is my chance. It was risky to follow her while passing through the tunnels, but while it opens wide at the terminal, I will safely jump down and through the shattered glass. There will be enough room to fit my body, and these idiots will be out of my way, too. Heart drumming, I coil up, ready to pounce at the first chance.

"Jump," I order my twin and the human sternly over my shoulder before turning my full focus on the incoming station.

A bright light blinds me momentarily when we turn the bend in the tunnel. Advertisements flicker on the left wall, changing too fast to be properly seen. The train's horn shrieks again, bursting my ear drums, and I flinch, a muscle pinching in my neck. As soon as we enter the wide space, Satanael throws himself at the tiled floor of the terminal. I spring forward, latching onto the spot I saw Helena last and swinging my body to the side of the train right over the broken window. A weight hits me in the gut, and my fingers slip from the flimsy grip I have on the metal.

My eyes lock on Helena before I'm yanked back at the open station like someone is pulling a string attached to me.

Her wide green irises are burned into my retinas when my back slams on the tiled floor, and the air is pushed from my lungs.

The train zooms by, leaving just the shrill sound of the horn behind before I can clear my head.

Chapter Twenty-Two

HELENA

A fresh torrent of tears roll down my face when I see Raphael bloody and barely clinging to life. It takes me a long moment to collect myself because of all the emotions choking me, and once I do, I'm finally able to move.

"Raphael." My broken whisper has him struggling to lift himself.

"Hel." Rasping my name, his arm jolts and slips over the blood-covered floor.

On hands and knees, I scramble toward him and help lift him until he is propped on the side of the seats. Cuts and bruises pepper his skin, turning it unrecognizable, so I lean my forehead on his shoulder as gently as I can and cry. Deep ugly sobs are wrenched from my chest.

"Why"—A wet cough shakes his whole body—"are you … here?"

"The same reason you are." Me wailing like a child is not going to help keep him alive. I pull back, wiping my tears with the back of my hand. "What do I do, Raphael?"

I think he is trying to laugh at me, but I can't be sure

because blood is spraying from his lips and dribbling down his chin. Panic is doing its best to strangle me, but I refuse to let it. I can freak the hell out later, maybe even kick the Archangel in his pearly whites, but I have to keep him alive so I can do that.

"Smart thinking to break the window." Maybe if I stroke his ego, he will work with me instead of against me, right? I mean all these males are as arrogant as they come.

"Not on purpose." Another chuckle, and he is coughing until his chest rattles with a wet sound.

"Easy there, Archangel." Shuffling closer on my knees, I drag his upper body to my chest and wrap my arms around him. "I think I told you once or twice that you are not allowed to die on my watch. Unless I kill you, of course." My attempt at humor works.

"How can I forget?" I don't like the defeated sigh that comes from him.

"Listen, I need you to tell me how to heal you, okay?" With a shaking hand, I push away some of the strands that are stuck to his face. "Just enough for you to help me lift you and push you out the window." That was the wrong choice of words because his body jerks in my hold, spasming. "It's me, Raphael; it's Helena." Reassurances rush through my lips, but they all jumble together when he tries to drag himself away from me.

How did I forget that the jinn tricked him once already by wearing my face? And here I am after he nearly died telling him I want to push him out a window. I'm so dumb sometimes. No wonder Eric thinks he has to hover around me in case I do something stupid and kill myself in the process. Jumping on a moving train and through a broken window at who knows how many miles per hour notwithstanding.

"No." Raphael pushes at my arms weakly.

"Please, Raphael. It's me, I swear it. What I was trying to say is, the train is not going to stop. We need to get out of here stat before it reaches the end of the rail line and both of us die here." Burying my face in his hair, I choke out, "Please tell me how to heal you."

At least he is not fighting me anymore.

"You need your strength." Barely above a whisper, I almost miss what he says.

"We can rest for a while *after* I get us out of here." A long second passes, and when he doesn't reply, I shake him. "No sleeping, stay with me, or I'll enjoy slapping your face."

"Go."

"Like hell I'm going to go anywhere without you." Since there will be no help from him, I will have to drag his ass to the window and through the damn thing, too.

Leaning him forward takes more effort than I like to admit, but I manage to almost fold him in half so I can stand. Holding onto his shoulders, I rubberneck to see where we are, thankful when only blurry walls of the tunnel show through the glass. The Archangel groans, the sound so full of pain my heart hurts for him.

"Here goes nothing." Clenching my teeth, I curl my forearms under his armpits and pull.

He slides a quarter of an inch before my boot slips on the blood, and I land on my ass. Actually, on my tail, to be precise. Stars burst in front of my eyes.

Cursing up a storm and using enough colorful words to make a sailor blush, I yank, huff, and puff with very little to show for it. Why is he so freaking heavy? Is he sagging limply on purpose to force me to leave him behind and run? Knowing the martyr Raphael thinks himself to be, I almost believe that that's what he is doing.

"Raphael, hear me good right now." Each word is pushed through clenched teeth. "I'm dragging your ass off this train if it's the last thing I do. With or without your help. If you don't do everything you can to make it easier for me, however, you'll regret it when I do get us out of this death trap." Sucking in a much-needed breath, I finish with a firm, "Am I clear?"

With a barely perceptible bob of his head, he says nothing but puts in some effort, as well. I half drag, half wiggle the Archangel over the blood and shards of glass. Glancing at his back where parts of it are cut so deep I can see the white of a bone peeking through the gash, I tear my eyes away, somehow reaching the wider area where wind whistles through the broken window.

Panting, I press my hands on my thighs, bending over. "I'll need you to stand up." Sounding like a bitch is inevitable. "You can use me as a crutch, but I must have you on your feet for this to work."

My heart stutters when a thumping from above us tells me the others are moving. Shit, the station must be coming, and if we miss it, who knows if there will be another opportunity? For all I know, after this one, there will be a wall that we will be ramming through. Whatever complaints Raphael has, he will have to keep them to himself because we were getting off on the next station, like it or not.

I crouch next to him and throw his arm over my shoulders. With one of mine wrapped around his waist and the other extended to hold onto the seat that is closest, I wiggle until I'm as lodged under him as I can possibly be. "On three, I need you to push. Raphael." My snap has his eyelashes fluttering, and he blinks, glancing around like he has no idea where he is. "I'm lifting you, so I need you to push to your feet as hard as you can. We have no time. On three."

"Very well."

"One." I lock my knees. "Two ... and three."

Shoving as hard as I can, I strain my back, but we finally end up standing and swaying like drunks in the empty carriage. With a death grip on the seats, I shuffle us until we face the gap where the window is broken. Raphael leans more and more on me with every breath, his eyelids drooping.

The darkness of the tunnel lightens, speeding up my heartbeat.

Twisting to the side, I manhandle the Archangel until he is as close as I can get him to the windowsill, and then I hold my breath while I wait. By the time all the shadows are gone, my lungs are screaming at me, but I don't dare blink.

Lights flood the carriage.

Flipping so we are face to face, I step back from Raphael before hunching down and ramming my shoulder at his chiseled, bruised abs. He jerks, his back bending and passing through the gap just as a dark shadow blocks our escape. The Archangel slams into the body that pops out of nowhere, and they both fly inside the well-lit station.

My eyes lock on Eric's for a split second before he and Raphael tumble on the tiled platform.

I suck in a startled breath.

And dive through the broken window after them.

Chapter Twenty-Three

HELENA

While I roll over the platform, my head cracking like a walnut across the tiles, I can't help but ask myself if there will ever be one week where I don't find myself in some crazy life-and-death situation. It doesn't need to be a month, or fates forbid half a year.

Just one fucking week without almost bleeding out, someone trying to kill me, or landing my ass in actual Hell.

One.

My body smacks into someone's legs, and it stops my trajectory on a pained groan. I'm pretty sure I have a concussion. Acid fills my mouth when voices echo and bounce around in my skull, where my brain is mushed enough to pretend it's soup. But since there is no rest for the wicked, I crack my eyes open a sliver so the light doesn't stab my retinas, flipping to crawl in search of Raphael.

If my brain was a functioning organ and not mashed potatoes, I would know that the others are standing around me, and they are more suited to helping the Archangel than

133

me. But it's not, plus I am too stubborn for my own good. Eric is right about that one. My toddler impersonation is short-lived, however.

Arms I'd recognize even if I was dead pluck me off the floor and lift me to a rock-hard chest. Eric's scent fills my nose, and the bile doesn't bubble up past my firmly pressed lips, thank everything holy. With a lot of blinking and many harsh exhales through my flaring nostrils, I finally bring his furious, very handsome face into view.

"He is alive." My choked rasp makes a muscle jump on one side of his jaw.

"I can see that."

"Don't growl, Eric. My head hurts." I think it's my father who snort-cough-chuckles in the background.

My mate glares at me.

I grin.

Well, I think I'm grinning, but I probably only manage to look constipated. My stomach is churning violently, and two times I come very close to emptying all the contents over both of us, but it finally settles after a moment. Eric just holds me without a word, but I don't miss the murder sparkling in his emerald irises.

Sensing I can talk without puking, I turn my head to the side to see where the rest are standing. "Is he going to be okay?"

Satanael looks up at me from his crouch next to Raphael's body lying over the white, dirty tiles. Beelzebub and Colt are kneeling too, while George looms over them, his skin as pale as a ghost and his hair sticking in all directions. Pride has my chest puffing out when I see my hunter friend standing tall—blanched or not—and keeping up with the supernatural creatures.

"In a moment." My father goes back to what he is doing, and I see the red glow emanating from his hands right before they sink inside the Archangel.

"He doesn't like that," I murmur for Eric's ears only, reminding him how skittish Raphael was in the past about being healed by Hell's energy.

"Well, he can suck it up," Eric snaps, and my hand moves before I can stop it.

I slap him.

Not that it does anything. His scowl is still firmly in place, and he stares at me unblinking with a muscle in the corner of his jaw ticking like an old-fashioned clock. "He almost died for me."

"And you thought it was a great idea to repay his sacrifice by jumping headfirst onto a moving train. Is that it?"

"Yes, that is it. And as you can see, everyone survived it." His features darken more, and I place my hand on his cheek, grazing his cheekbone with my thumb. "I would've done the same for you, Eric." His mouth opens, but I press my fingers over it to shush him. "For all of you."

Whatever was going to come out through his lips ends up being a harsh breath. "I thought him dying would surely kill you."

"I have a feeling I didn't feel his injuries because of the shock and the crippling thought that he died because of me." Wiggling to get more comfortable in his arms, I don't ask him to put me down. I can tell he needs to hold me close for his sanity's sake. "I feel them now, though."

"Good. Maybe that will teach you to stop doing this, Helena. I hoped ..." A lock of hair falls over his face when he shakes his head. "I honestly thought having the two of us tied to you would put a stop to this nonsense."

"Would you have seriously just left him without knowing his fate if you were able to jump on that train first?" When he doesn't even blink, I have my answer. "I didn't think so."

A torrent of curses rings around us, and we turn to see Raphael sit up, his hands running over his chest and everywhere he can reach on his back. For an Archangel, he sure can surprise us with his vocabulary from time to time.

"Helena." His head swivels around, and Satanael draws back so Raphael can see me. "It was you." He exhales a breath of relief. "I didn't hallucinate."

"Nope. Just me and my crazy self dragging your ass where it belongs. No jumping off this insane wagon, Raphael. Sorry. If I have to deal with this shit, so do you." My finger points at him in accusation. "What the fuck were you thinking?" It actually wasn't his fault since there was no room for him to fit in the narrow space, but my irrational mashed potato brain doesn't care.

"I have learned my lesson." He is still black and blue but no longer bleeding. "It will not happen again." One corner of his mouth twitches for a split second. If I would've blinked, I wouldn't have seen it.

Satanael gives the Archangel such a loaded look I swear I could touch it if I reach my fingers between them. Raphael's cheekbones turn a pale shade of rose, and Eric growls deep in his chest. My mouth opens to ask what it's about since I hate being out of the loop with something that's obviously common knowledge to everyone, but the question stays stuck on my tongue.

My father's head whips to the side, and he lifts his chin, inhaling deeply like a dog sniffing a fresh bone. Eric stiffens, tightening his arms under me and twisting around as if a horde of demons is rushing at us. The line of stairs leading toward the surface is empty like a ghost town, and confusion has me poking my mate in the chest.

"What's going on?" His answer is to glance at Satanael. I do, too, with an expectant expression all over my face.

"We are close," he tells me absentmindedly.

It takes a second to remember the heavenly light he mentioned what feels like ten lifetimes ago. With the adrenaline rush that came from seeing Raphael whisked away and thinking he was dead, crawling over a moving train, and jumping out of one with a half-dead Archangel draped over my shoulders, I totally forgot why we were still playing rats inside the MARTA network of tunnels.

"Well, let's go find it." My insistent tapping has Eric dropping my feet to the floor. "I don't know about the rest of you, but I don't want to be underground anymore."

A chorus of grumbled agreements echoes around us, and we all spring into action toward the same damn tunnel the train zipped through behind Satanael. My father takes the lead again with his nose up in the air. Despite all my reluctance, my feet don't falter when we drop on the tracks. I do wait for Raphael to join me before moving forward, however.

"You good?" My whispered question has Eric growling again, but the Archangel gives me the full weight of his gaze.

"I am, thanks to you." My smile mimics his.

"Let's go find this thing and get the hell out of here. This part should be easy."

We plunge into the darkness again without the soft glow from Raphael. I don't dare mention it because there is no question in my mind that he is barely able to stand on his feet. We will make do without him exerting himself just so we don't trip. I don't comment when he falls behind us and takes the rear, either. Maybe he needs time to think about what happened. Linking my fingers through Eric's, I square my shoulders.

I should know from experience that nothing in my life is ever easy.

I have no idea why I even said it to Raphael.

Chapter Twenty-Four

ERIC

"Why does it feel like we've been stuck walking through this tunnel for months?" Helena says, her tone so low I think she might be talking more to herself than me.

"Because danger follows you like you are on a personal mission to keep its existence alive," I answer regardless, still pissed about the whole jumping-on-a-moving-train situation.

It's not like I don't get it.

As soon as I saw her leap on it over Beelzebub's shoulder while crammed in the claustrophobic closet, my mind followed without any doubts creeping in as to whether it was a smart idea or not. From day one, Helena was a spur-of-the-moment decision maker, and most of the time, I'm all for it. Not always though.

"What do you think we are going to find?" Not looking at me, she changes the subject and ignores my comment.

I shrug. "Does it matter?"

"Of course, it matters. We've been cleaning up the city, but eventually, we need to set up some boundaries and rules to be followed. Everyone mingles and gets along for the time being because they are all still freaked out about the skies and the ground opening up to free creatures of their imagination to roam their world. And they accept them ... for now." Blowing a breath through pursed lips, she shakes her head. "How long do you think that's going to last?"

"Okay." I drag the word out, not understanding where she's going with it.

"Whatever we find may have an impact on that?" Waving a hand in front of her in annoyance, she glances at me from the corner of her eye. "Look at us. We are bloody and beaten just trying to find it and see what it is. If they went to so much trouble to hide it, maybe it's not meant to be discovered."

My feet plant on the ground, and I pull her to a stop with me. Turning to face me, she cocks an eyebrow at my sudden reluctance to keep going.

"Let me get this straight. You think it's better to leave something that might be important so you can turn around and pretend it's not here? In *your* Atlanta, as you love reminding all of us."

"Why is it so hard for you to believe that I'm not that big of an idiot?" Tugging her hand from mine, she whirls around so she can walk away from me.

I don't think so.

"Because if there is the slightest possibility this is a danger to the humans, you are all over it. No matter how much it pains me, you'll never turn your back on them. On anyone, really. So, what's going on?" Nipping at her heels, I feel really confused. This is not my mate.

She doesn't just walk away.

Helena may cause realms to collide, and she may jump headfirst into the open mouth of a monster without thinking twice about how any of us feel about it—as long as the useless humans are safe in their miserable lives—but I'm missing something major here. I can taste it.

The others are preoccupied checking everything around us so we don't have any more surprises of the almost-dead variety and pay us no mind. Raphael is lost in his own thoughts, shuffling his feet behind us, although he might still be woozy from his ordeal. That's why they all tense and snap to attention when she rounds on me with a strangled shout.

"Because I can't do this anymore, Eric." There is a wild glint in her wide eyes, and her fists are clenched. "We have been through so much just to be able to stand here alive and breathing. *I* have been through so much. Excuse me if I don't want to watch any of you die on the off chance that all of it will work out somehow. What if I can't do anything to stop it next time?"

Ah, it's still about the Archangel.

I do want to turn around and punch his mug.

"We will deal with everything as it comes, Hel." After a few protests, she allows me to pull her to my chest and wrap her in my arms. "One thing at a time. You and I, if that's how it'll be. I will not let you down, and you have my word on that."

"I know"—Her voice is muffled in my chest, but she does hug me back—"you'll just growl about it as usual. I keep telling you it scares the shit out of people."

My chuckle makes her sigh, and she sags in my arms. I wish I can wrap her in a bubble and hide her somewhere where no one and nothing can find her. Staying on our toes and dodging death left and right is all good and well, but when is enough, enough? Helena is not just physically stretched thin. Her mental wellbeing has been pushed way beyond its limit for a while now. One fight after another takes a toll on anyone.

I tell her as much.

"No, I'm fine." I can tell she doesn't believe it. "I mean, do I like it? Maybe the stabby parts, but no, I don't enjoy going from one clusterfuck to another. Oh well, it is what it is. I'll deal."

"You two will have to *deal* sooner rather than later," Satanael grumbles, and we both turn his way, startled.

We've been walking for almost half an hour after the train fiasco with nothing to show for it. My skin is too tight having Helena here longer than necessary. I'm all for getting it done as fast as we can so I can whisk her away.

"It's the strongest here." With his hands on his hips, Satanael spins in a slow circle, his brow pinched.

The human hunter points the flashlight he's been using at the walls to break the darkness. A circle of yellow light zigzags side to side and up and down, searching for an entrance. My twin and Beelzebub straddle the low railing and start running their hands over the concrete when no door can be seen anywhere.

"How sure are you?" Colt grumbles, grimacing and adjusting himself so his balls don't get pinched by the thin railing. "Maybe further down because there is nothing here."

"I am certain we are on top of it." Satanael doesn't like being told he doesn't know what he is doing. My brother should know that.

"Human," Raphael pipes in absentmindedly, "check the ceiling."

The light jumps to the roof, moving from one side to the other slowly like that will help somehow. Helena steps away from me, and as much as I hate it, I leave her to help the others. After a few minutes of petting walls like they are our lovers, we are all grumbling and frustrated because, as Colt said, there is absolutely nothing here. I give up and turn to grab my mate so we can keep moving. My heart punches my ribs hard when I don't see her straight away. Eyes frantically darting everywhere all at once, I almost miss her, but then I see her standing near Raphael, who is frozen like a statue staring at the ground. Following his gaze, I find her.

On her hands and knees, Helena is pressing her cheek on the grime and who-knows-what-else-covered ground. Thinking she is unwell, I trip over the fucking railing and pitch forward before I right myself so I can go pick her up. Why is the prick just standing there watching her like she's an insect under his boot?

"Get out of my way." The Archangel stumbles with an exclaimed protest when I shove hard on his chest.

I reach for Helena.

"No wait," my mate hisses, and my hand freezes above her shoulder. Her gaze flicks to my face. "Just wait."

"What are you doing?"

Is this some sort of stretching exercise because she is sore? I mean, I've seen her do yoga before she goes through her routine to keep herself flexible so she can fight, but doing it here? The need to pick her up or let her be war within me.

"Listening," she says, her words barely above a whisper.

"To what?" I feel dumber than a box of rocks.

"A train." There is no mistaking the frustration in her tone.

I stiffen, my entire body locking.

She must notice my reaction because she scrambles to her feet, her jerky movements only feeding my anxiety at the though of her being in danger once again.

"There is no train." Her reassurance comes out like a jumbled mess. "I was just listening while you guys are searching for a door in case we need to scram, you know?" Her sheepish look calms me slightly. "If you press your ear on the tracks, you can hear a train coming before you see it."

Scrubbing a hand over my face, I exhale loudly. There is no need for anyone to attack us because this female will be the death of me. Is it possible for someone like me to die from a heart attack? Helena sure as hell is putting it to a very thorough test.

"What do you know?" Beelzebub mutters before laughing gleefully. "Well, well, what have we here?"

Chapter Twenty-Five

HELENA

Maybe it was dumb to stick my ass in the air to listen if another killer train is coming, but they can't blame me for it. Fear was a living thing twisting my insides, and Raphael's sad, golden irises were tormenting me in the back of my mind like the moment he was ripped away right in front of me. My throat tight and clogged with emotions, I follow Eric to where Beelzebub is pointing at a part of the wall, and he's wearing the biggest grin I've ever seen on his face.

"I don't see it." All of them ignore my comment, so I bend my head to search the floor.

Is it really an object so small that I can't spot it right away? My feet fidget where I'm standing from impatience and tension coiling my body because of the awkward, uncomfortable silence between Raphael and me when Eric walked away. Yes, I was angry for what the Archangel did, but I wasn't holding it against him.

I would've done the same.

Why is there this heavy, pregnant air around us when we stand close then?

"Fucking wards," Eric spits to the side, and his fist slams into the portion of the wall they are examining like it's the greatest thing after sliced bread.

That has my full attention.

"There is a door there." My heartbeat picks up, and I saddle closer to the narrow path, wrapping my fingers around the cold railing so I can lean in and see better.

"Step aside, Hel." My mate nudges me when he steps back a couple of feet. "Let's break them and get the hell out of here. I've had enough bullshit."

Latching onto his forearm, I tug him back. "There could be traps set, Eric. What do you think you are doing?"

"Triggering them before you decide to go for it," he answers me flatly with a pointed look.

I flinch.

Okay, fine. I deserve that, but he really doesn't need to be a jerk about it. It's not like I do things on purpose. With my lips pressed in a firm line, I nod at him and give him space to do … whatever he is planning to do. Raphael's hand comes to my lower back in comfort, not touching but close enough that I can feel the heat of his skin. Heart stuttering, I take a deep breath.

"We can break through them, she-devil." Colt smirks at me, but it doesn't reach his eyes. "I'll let you have dibs on whatever needs stabbing inside."

"Deal." It does make me feel better even when I know they are placing the girl in the naughty corner so she doesn't get in their way. Any other time, I'll be in their faces with my dagger at their throats. Not today.

For a good twenty minutes, they blast the portion of the wall with their powers, with fists, shoulders, and even kicks. It remains just a wall, although if it was the real thing, they would've created a hole as big as a canyon by now the way they were going at it.

"It'll be easier if I just bleed on it." My offhanded comment has them gawking at me. I shrug. "I'm just saying. So far, it has proven very effective, but what do I know? Carry on."

They all turn at once and continue pummeling the wards, as well as whatever is hidden by them. George is the one who stands to the side with a thoughtful look pinching his face. I smile tightly at him, and with a glance to make sure the males are occupied, he slides to stand shoulder to shoulder with me.

"I'll do it," ,y hunter friend says from the corner of his mouth, not taking his eyes off the group of pissed-off demons and an Archangel. "Give me your blood. I'll smear it on the cursed wall."

"Give it to you how?" Mumbling just as low, I straighten from my slump. "You are not touching the dagger."

I've had enough shit to last me ten lifetimes when it comes to my weapon and the way it calls to everyone to take it. Not even Eric wants to go anywhere near it.

"Just cut off my hand and grab it." His hiss makes me want to slap myself.

Hanging around all these arrogant creatures—despite the fact that I was one too—has me thinking like them lately. I prided myself on being scrappy and thinking on my feet, but now I'm dumbly standing to the side and relying on brute strength. Eyeing the guys, I drop my hand to the hilt of my dagger and pull it out as inconspicuously as I can. One jerk down my opposite palm, and warm fluid fills my closed fist. If I was human, it'd take ages for it to heal, but thankfully I am not. The wound will close in a few seconds.

I take George's hand, smearing as much of it as possible over his palm.

He doesn't mingle or wait. Dropping my grip on him, he darts at the gathered males, shoulders between them, and slaps his hand on the wall with a loud, wet smack. My skin prickles before I can register what is happening, and the next thing I know, I'm flying back along with everyone else. A blast of power slams into us, throwing us off with a resounding boom. All the air exits my lungs when I hit the opposite wall hard, the back of my head cracking on it. Stars bloom in my vision, and my ears thunder worse than when the train zipped in front of me.

With a shake of my head, I lift on my hands and knees, panting while the tunnel swims and warps around me, and bile threatens to push all the contents of my stomach out. This is getting old. I'm tired of being tossed around like yesterday's dirty underwear. The others get up too, their lips curled in snarls and glares firmly in place. I avoid looking directly at Eric, but I do breathe a sigh of relief when George pops his head up.

"We should've listened to Helena from the start." Colt, of all people, snorts, his voice coming muffled like he is talking underwater.

Whatever the others had to say is lost in the startled shouts when the now revealed door bursts open, and three demons, all eight feet tall with large sets of horns, step out of it. No one hesitates, and they collide with my guys in a loud crash of flesh hitting flesh. I stumble to my feet when a passing shadow catches my eye behind the full-on brawl in the middle of the tunnel. From the faint glow through the open doorway, I see the edge of fabric disappearing to the side.

Someone else is there.

Roars, screams, and shouts echo around me, but my gaze is locked on that door and I have no intention of getting sidetracked. Pulling my dagger out for the second time in so many minutes, I inch around the fight, not daring to blink in case whoever is there makes a run for it. Lucky the guys are preoccupied because I manage to slip in before they see what I'm doing.

Or unlucky, as the case may be.

I almost drop my weapon when a set of eyes exactly like mine lock on my gaze.

"Mom?" The word passes as soft as a breath through my lips.

Chapter Twenty-Six

HELENA

A smile as cold and as scary as a shark staring you in the face while it's preparing to eat you greets me. A chill slithers up and down my spine, but I'm frozen in place, and all the demons in all the worlds can't move me from this spot. The roof can drop on my head, and I'll still gape at the woman standing proud to face me.

It's like looking in the mirror.

The differences become obvious a second later, but the initial reaction of having Zadkiel in front of me scrambles my brain. The similar bone structure of her face, as well as the shape of her mouth and eyes, startles me. Her nose is slightly more pointed, and a waterfall of midnight black hair cascades over her shoulders to the small of her back. Dressed in black, what seem to be leggings and a tight black long-sleeved top, she is taller than me by a few inches, and thinner, as well. Where my hips are round and my thighs are, as I love to say, chunky, she is a perfectly formed lean killing machine.

But those eyes.

I believe that I'm more stunned by the fact that she is looking down her nose at me like I'm dirt under her shoe than anything else. I thought when, and if, I found her, she'd be chained and barely clinging to life just like Satanael. The chains that held my father prisoner are still fresh in my mind.

"Helena." Voice as beguiling as a siren, she juts her hip to the side. "We finally meet."

I'll bet my newly acquired tail and wings she is not happy about that little fact. Confused as fuck, I open my mouth and then close it, the fighting from behind me giving the whole situation some nightmarish quality. In the hopes of regaining my composure, I glance around her at the room, which is three times the size of the one we had available when running for our lives. Naked walls meet my eyes, until I stop on the heap on the floor with glowing chains around it. Blinking fast so I can understand what I'm seeing, my heart punches at the roof of my mouth before splattering at my feet.

Lucifer, his face unrecognizable from all the swelling and bruising, hangs limply behind my mother, a large pool of dark blood forming a small lake under him. Streaks of gold shimmer through it, and he looks much larger—well, thicker than I remember. That's until he groans faintly, slipping further down into the lump of twisted limbs, and I see the blond strands of hair from behind him.

Michael.

They are tied together back to back by the glowing chains, and seeing them like that brings all the fury I try so hard to keep pushed down so I don't lose my mind to the surface. My eyes snap back to my mother's face, and she's smirking at me now, so I grind my teeth while tightening my hold on the dagger. Why is she all smiles and arrogance while Lucifer and Michael are bleeding out on the floor?

"You are not Zadkiel, are you?" My knees bend slightly, and I lift my weapon.

"Come now, Helena." Her long, graceful fingers flick a strand of silky hair over her shoulder. "No need to insult each other is there?"

Rage-filled roars follow her snotty comment, and dread fills my belly. It sounds like more demons have joined the fight from somewhere in the tunnels.

"Jinn," I spit the word in disgust.

Very rooky of me to think my mother will be enjoying life while waiting for me to find her, dressed like she is going to a club, and completely unharmed. Instead of gawking like a dumbass, I need to introduce her to the pointy bit of my dagger and get Lucifer and Michael out of here. Now.

"It's very difficult for you to understand, isn't it." When I say nothing, she continues with her monologue. "But"—Her finger comes up—"you really are difficult to kill. I'll give you that much. My bloodline is stronger in you than I originally expected."

Unwilling to play anymore games, I jump at her, slashing with my blade. The dagger passes a hairsbreadth away from her torso when she hunches back, sucking her stomach in. Using the momentum, I spin, kicking out and managing to catch her on the side. Stumbling, she laughs, the sound like crystal shards falling over marble. She goes as far as tsking at me with a wide grin plastered on her face.

"Now, now, child." More giggles follow, and I want to scream. "Is this how you greet your mother?"

"You are not my mother," I snarl, circling her.

If I can get between her and the two males chained to the wall, I'll hold her back until the others join us. That's my plan anyway, as pathetic as it is. Unfortunately, the fight outside in the tunnel doesn't sound like it'll end anytime soon, so I don't have another choice. Unless I end up killing the jinn. That makes me smile.

"Am I not?" the Zadkiel wannabe moves in sync with me. "However did you figure that out?"

"It didn't work for your buddies when they tried pretending they were Michael, Eric, and even me. They all died." My bared teeth make a line form between her perfectly shaped eyebrows. "Now it's your turn."

Pouncing, I jab the dagger in her shoulder. What I said must've really gotten her attention because she doesn't duck or twist away from it. The blade embeds in her flesh until it hits bone, and the runes flare brightly. A shrill scream bursts through her lips, and the palm of her hand connects to my chest. The impact almost caves my ribcage in before I fly back and hit the wall next to Lucifer and Michael.

"You insolent child," she snarls, clutching her shoulder.

"Zadkiel …" one of the chained males mumbles, but I would've missed it if I wasn't kneeling next to them.

"It's a jinn." Pushing through clenched teeth, I try to get up, but the next words take all my strength.

"It's Zadkiel …" My head snaps, and I lock onto Lucifer's one eye dull from pain.

All the blood curdles in my veins.

"No." My voice comes from somewhere in the distance as my legs crumple under me.

Zadkiel, the real one and not a jinn pretending to be her like I thought, glares at me from across the room with harted burning in her eyes. There is nothing in them but a hungry abyss ready to devour me whole. How is this possible? She tried to save me by giving me to Raphael and the Order, didn't she? Satanael himself said that she would go to great lengths to protect me. My thoughts must show on my face because her sneer is back.

"Poor Helena. She finally understands that all this is not about her." Unable to keep her gaze unless I puke, I fasten my eyes on her wounded shoulder. Seeing the golden blood dripping through her fingers stabs me like a hot poker in the chest.

"Why?" I breathe, the words ripped from me despite my desire to stay silent. I don't owe her anything. "How could you?"

"None of this would've happened if you just stayed with that measly human and died in one of your hunts." Her snarl is more animal than Archangel. How the fuck is this creature an angel? "When I came to make sure you stayed out of my way, my dagger dropped, and that imbecile gave it to you."

"Run ..." Lucifer whispers, but I can't move an inch. I just stare at her numbly.

"Why?" I hear myself ask again faintly.

"For power, you cretin." Her scream rings in my ears. "Why else wold I suffer all this idiocy and that disgusting demon's touch."

I suck in a breath when Raphael fills the doorway behind her, his already pale face blanching of all color. My mouth opens so I can scream at him to run, but I'm too late.

"Zadkiel?" His shocked whisper has her whirling around to face him.

"You." With a snarl, she throws herself at him, and hands slick with her blood wrap around his neck.

"No!" My shriek follows them through the door.

Chapter Twenty-Seven

RAPHAEL

Crippling shock has me frozen while Zadkiel squeezes for all she is worth in her attempt to choke me to death. I do not fight back or even try to remove her grip on my neck because I'm stunned by the golden blood drenching her shirt. Lungs burning and heart hammering at my protesting ribs from her weight, my gaze travels over her shoulder when Helena appears in the doorway. It breaks something in me to see the heart-wrenching sorrow on her face, but to go to her, I need to not die first.

Nothing makes sense.

When I realize we are fighting too long like the hellspawn is trying to keep us occupied instead of killing us, I search for Helena. Not seeing her anywhere has me separating from the others and rushing into the room only to find, not just my charge, but Zadkiel, too.

"Raphael." Helena's broken cry clears the cobwebs assaulting my brain, and wiggling my fingers between Zadkiel's, I wrench her hands off me. Her enraged scream makes me flinch, and I throw her to the side.

155

Still dazed, I jump to my feet and take a step toward Helena. The only warning is the widening of her green eyes and the terror I see in them. Whirling around, I raise my hand in time to block the short sword that would've carved me in half. The blade sinks in my forearm, and my snarl has Zadkiel yanking it out and jumping back.

"Good to see you, Raphael." The female, who I've thought about for decades and done things for that make me ashamed to wear a pair of wings, stares at me like I'm her enemy.

"What is the meaning of this, Zadkiel?" Surprised I sound calm, I stand between the two females.

There is only a handful of the higher-class demons left battling on the other side of the tunnel. I catch Eric darting glances toward his mate, but if he sees me standing here, he will finish the fight knowing I will protect Helena with my life. Even from her own mother.

Good thing Satanael hasn't seen what is happening away from the horned attackers.

"It must be nice for you to enter and leave Heaven as you please." Zadkiel throws a cursory look over her shoulder, her sword held at the ready with the tip pointed my way. My frown must clue her in to confused I am. "Some of us were unworthy, as you see."

"Don't be absurd, lower your weapon. You are the Mercy of God, and that means you are worthy." I sound hollow to my own ears. "I thought you were dead."

"How convenient for all of you." Sneering, she slashes at me, and we spin, twisting and turning until she scores another hit. Blood runs down my thigh, filling my boot. "You think the jinn did this? That those pathetic creatures could come up with such a brilliant plan? If it wasn't for you, everything would've passed smoothly."

"Put the sword down and we can talk." Hands to my sides in hopes to calm her, I lock my gaze on hers. "I do not know what happened to you, Zadkiel, but we can get past it. You trusted me once, so I need you to believe in me again."

Indecision flickers in those irises I know too well. I've gazed at them many centuries wondering if I will ever hold her in my embrace as a male holds a female and not just a friend to lend a shoulder and an ear. The same Zadkiel stands before me now with my blood on her sword. Same, yet so very different. Whatever she was about to say never reaches my ears when Helena steps next to me.

"I see." Zadkiel's sneer turns into a chilling glare. "How predictable."

"What the fuck is your problem?" Helena, to my chagrin, steps ahead of me, placing me at her back. Her dagger points right at her mother's face. "You want Raphael, bitch? You'll have to go through me first."

"With pleasure."

The two females collide, blades arching in the fray of kicking limbs and long strands of hair flying around them like sheets of silk on a strong breeze. Dread fills me, but I stay rooted to the spot, fearful I will hurt one or the other without attempting to if I get involved.

"Zadkiel, stop this. She is your daughter." My desperate attempt to separate them falls on deaf ears. For a moment.

"All of this is because of her." I stiffen when she shouts. "When she dies, time will reset itself." Slashing with her sword, she almost stabs Helena in the back. "Everything will go back the way it was. All my mistakes forgotten." Judging by the look of disdain, Zadkiel believes Helena is a mistake.

I might be undecided on whether or not to step between a mother and daughter, but Satanael does not have the same shortcomings. As soon as the last demon drops, the other males turn to the one-on-one battle playing out a foot from where I'm uselessly standing.

"I will drink your blood, Zadkiel, and feast on your bone marrow if a hair is missing on her head." Satanael's roar rattles the whole tunnel.

Everything happens so fast my brain cannot register who moves where.

Zadkiel jumps away from her daughter, her dark hair swirling around her head, and with one furious look at Satanael, she bolts down the tunnel. He tries to give chase, but Helena's call stops him, and he pants like a raging bull in the middle of the tracks glaring at the darkness like he can will her back with his mind. Eric and the others rush to Helena, their hands fleeting around her body in their desperate attempt to check for injuries.

"I found Lucifer and Michael. They need us more than we need her dead. Her time will come." Her voice breaks, but she doesn't let the tears brimming in her eyes fall.

I just stand.

Alone and lost with a gaping hole widening inside me.

How could this be?

What in all the heavens has Zadkiel gotten herself into.

I refuse to believe she is behind all the bloodshed, all the hurt and pain everyone around me has suffered. There must be something I'm missing. I cannot turn my back on the female I love.

My eyes slowly move to Helena, and an invisible fist closes around my throat. I do love Zadkiel.

Don't I?

Chapter Twenty-Eight

HELENA

"I'm okay." Slapping Eric's hand away, I sigh.

We've been back at the safe house for a while now. I'm pretty sure that more than twenty-four hours were lost while we walked the tunnels, but in all the crazy, at least Lucifer and Michael were found. The wards dulled Michael's essence, but not enough to hide him from my father. Both of them are sleeping, but at least they will live.

"You need to wash that blood off you and rest, Hel." Wrapping me in a hug, he tucks my head under his chin. "They're not going anywhere. Both of them will still be here when you are done."

"I want to eat his face," Narsi hisses from where he is hugging my leg, his narrowed eye sockets locked on poor Michael.

"I told you it's not the same Michael, Narsi." With a groan, I tug on his wild curls to hold him back. "The asshole we hate was a jinn, not the real Archangel. This one is not evil." I hope I'm telling him the truth after what I lived through with my mother.

159

Speaking of which.

"How's Raphael doing?" Tilting my head back, I search Eric's face for a sign in case he decides to trick me into not going to find my friend.

"As good as he could possibly be after discovering the one he loved most of his existence is a murderous bitch." His mouth snaps shut, and his jaw tightens.

"I'll eat her face." Narsi preens, staring adoringly at Eric. He will love anyone as long as they let him munch on someone. I kick at him as a joke, which makes him pout.

"When we find her, I'll be happy to watch you eat her," I tell my sidekick to cheer him up before I nudge Eric. "I think you are right. I do need a shower."

And maybe everything will make more sense while I stand under the hot stream. Why my mother turned out to be a psycho—that definitely took me for a spin when I saw her—why Raphael didn't hold her down so we can take her with us to question her, and most of all, what was the nonsense she said about my death turning time back to erase her mistakes?

Stupidly I believe that because of what I am—and that's what everyone has been telling me so far—time will collapse with my death and all the realms and everything in them will no longer exist. As terrifying as that responsibility is, being used like a get-out-of-jail-free card to get a clean slate sounds worse. What am I? an Ace up her sleeve so she can fuck up people's lives and then walk away unsheathed?

I don't think so.

There is more to this new clucterfuck that is taking my life for a spin, but until I get my hands on Zadkiel—I refuse to refer to her as my mother after everything—all I can do is drown in my dread and pity for myself until I go insane. I should be used to this, right? I mean, first my adopted father hired Eric to kill me, and then the Order, who were my family, turned against me. Why is it shocking to find out the one who gave me life has hated me all this time?

When I first found out I had demon blood, I lost it, thinking that I was evil and whatnot. I wanted to die knowing Satanael—Satan—was my father, but the big guy turned out to have better parental skills than that psycho mother of mine. All his arrogance aside, of course.

"I would've joined you, but I have to meet with your father and the others. They are planning to start a full-blown search for you mo—for Zadkiel," Eric corrects himself fast when I narrow my eyes at him.

"Go." Shoving him gently I lift on my tiptoes and peck his lips. "When you are done, come join me. I'll probably be asleep for ten days after all the crazy."

"I have my ways of waking you up." His smoldering gaze sends butterflies in my belly.

"You do that." My tone is breathy, and with wet panties, I push him again. "The sooner you go, the sooner you'll keep your promise."

Mashing his mouth on mine, he steals my breath before stepping back. "Remember, neither my father nor Michael are going anywhere. They'll be here after you wash and rest."

"Aye, aye captain." I hold my smile until he turns a corner, and then I let it slip. "Narsi?"

Spinning on my heel, I act like I'm not just about to get myself and my sidekick into a ton of trouble. As predicted, he darts after me, looking up while bouncing on his small feet.

"How do you feel about investigating?"

"Narsi likes to eat," he tells me pointedly, then adds, "faces." As if I can ever forget what kind of diet he prefers.

"I'll make you a deal." Snatching his hand, I lead him toward my room. "I'll tell you what we need to find out, and if you help me ... you can have all the faces you want."

"Narsi loveeesss faces." I watch him run in excitement, unable to follow my even gait.

Dread weighs down my belly, but I don't see another way.

I will find Zadkiel with Narsi's help, and she will sing like a canary when she gets introduced to my dagger all over again. Only this time, she will not be coming face to face with a timid daughter searching for her mother.

Satanael will seem like cupid by the time I'm done with her.

She's about to see who the real Devil is.

And this devil, well ... she always gets her due.

Also by Maya Daniels

vinci-books.com/blackhand

They made me their weapon. Now, I'm aiming at them.

The Council spent a thousand years crafting the perfect assassin—
me. I played along… until they killed my friend. Now? I'm taking
them down one body at a time. With a vampire, a human, and a
shifter at my side, the Council's reign is about to end. They won't
see this coming.

Turn the page for a free preview…

Black Hand: Chapter One

I was unprepared.

I wasn't ready for the curve ball life was about to throw at me.

Nor did I anticipate what the fates had in store for the near future.

The tiny pinpricks of light reflected through the window of the plane, the city below the metal bird stretching over the hills as far as I could see. I mushed my face closer to get a better look, but the glass fogged from my breath. My stomach dropped when we lost altitude, the winds lashing at the plane making the last fifty minutes of the flight turbulent and unsettling. If it went down, it'd solve a lot of my problems. Although …

I was unprepared for that, as well.

I wanted to live.

My heart skipped a beat when the light blinked on above my head for the seatbelt, the loud chime echoing through my head like a gong going off. The plane was made for humans, not creatures like me with super-sensitive hearing. Being an *Atua* was seen as fiction in this world. They liked to call us vampires, but little did they know we were very much real, we lived among them, we manipulated their lives for our gain, and we had no remorse at all. Well, most of my kind didn't. I, on the other hand, was cursed ... or something. I cared a little too much.

I should've expected my reaction to get attention, but I did not. It would've saved me a lot of hassle if I didn't flinch like a rookie. Too late I noticed the flight attendant beelining my way with a look of determination on her face. Her hands were swinging by her body in fast, sharp jerks as her legs scrunched her skirt above her knees from her long strides. The woman was on a mission and there was no mistaking that.

You'd think she was about to fight a crocodile to save my life.

"You doing okay there, doll?" Her brown gaze locked on my face, the expression there telling me I'd better not lie to her, and her hairstyle with not a single hair out of line said, "Don't mess with me.".

"I'm good, thank you." Offering a small smile that was more a press of my lips than anything else, I stared at her chin. A bad habit I'd developed through the years so I could keep my eyes hidden. They gave away the fire scorching my insides from the anger I'd internalized for centuries. To humans they were just freaky, I guessed.

"She gets nervous when flying," Veronica chirped from next to me, shifting in her seat and flipping her blonde ponytail over her shoulder with a delicate hand. "She'll be fine as soon as we land."

"We are almost there." The Flight attendant gave me a

once over as if checking for tells that I wasn't being truthful. "Keep your seats up and put your seatbelts on. Around this time of the year, the winds don't make it easy for those that get jittery on a flight."

"Will do," we both piped in with tight smiles aimed at the attendant, and I turned to look out the window again because I was done talking. I heard her footsteps slowly walking away after about a minute, and she'd probably stared at the back of my head that whole time.

"Stay alert. You're slipping," Veronica murmured under her breath, her words too low for anyone but me to hear her. "Snap out of it before we have the same situation we had three years ago."

"Right." Ignoring her jab about my trip to the cages—where I spent an entire year in darkness with barely any blood to keep me alive—I kept my eyes glued to the glass, seeing nothing, though her words did send a ping straight through my gut. My fingers trailed over the inside of my left forearm, the phantom pain reminding me of the ripped flesh that used to be there regardless of the smooth skin covering it now. The cruel voices laughing and gloating at my pain while they teared my flesh were trying to drown me, but I clenched my jaw and pushed them away. I would not dwell on that now.

Not ever.

Immortality was seen as a blessing by humans, their lives spent dreaming of having eternity to do everything they wanted. They envied creatures they read about in books, creatures like me that kept their youth and roamed through centuries. What they didn't see was the ugly truth behind what we were. They were blind to all the suffering we went through while our physical bodies stayed the same, only memories of the pain left behind haunting our dreams.

And there wasn't even a scar to show for it.

Only memories.

Snatching my hand away, I tightened my fist and used the sharp bite of my nails to bring me out of that dark hole filled with misery. Nothing good ever came from dwelling on the past. Yet ... darting my gaze across the lights below us, I couldn't help the sigh that escaped me. I wished I was down there with them. I wished I belonged to their world instead of the hellish nightmare mine was. It was difficult to swallow the lump clogging my throat while my lashes fluttered to get rid of the burn behind my eyes. I would not cry. Looking back, I hadn't cried for years, and I had no intention to start now. No, I had a job to do.

"You need to move," Veronica mumbled as she turned to face me, her brown eyes full of pity. My lips pressed in a firm line of displeasure, but I couldn't blame my friend for feeling sorry for me. I was an emotional, pathetic fool most days, and what I was sent here to do would be just another thing to add to my nightmares. "Don't do anything stupid, Brooklyn, I beg of you. Not now."

A lock of fire-red hair fell over my eye and I blew it up in frustration. It wasn't like I planned to do stupid things, though the word stupid was debatable depending which perspective one used to look at things, of course. I just had issues with blindly following orders. Personally, I couldn't say needing more information before you took someone's life was stupid, but what did I know? According to those that ruled over my life, not much obviously.

"Bee?" Veronica squeezed my knee and brought me back to the present. "I can do it—"

"No, I got this." I didn't allow her to finish the sentence. She had done enough to cover for my little rebellions. I handled the cages. Veronica wouldn't last a week.

Plus, I had a plan.

A stupid one, of course.

"Forty minutes until landing," my friend reminded me, staring over the seat in front of her as she flattened invisible wrinkles on her pencil skirt.

Leave it to Veronica to be dressed to the nines no matter the situation. The black skirt she wore was paired with a silky champaign colored blouse that complimented her pale skin and blonde hair. With six-inch heels and her long legs folded primly to the side, she was ready to be on the cover of a magazine, not in an economy seat on a flight to Chicago. Or next to someone like me who was covered from head to toe in black leather, including the boots covering my feet. My fire-red hair and eerily bright green eyes were the only color anyone would ever see on me. I liked my clothing to match my mood, and it had been as dark as it could get for so long I couldn't remember it ever being any different.

My body jerked forward when one of the children sitting behind me kicked at the back of my seat, throwing another tantrum when his mother told him to put his seat-belt on. The poor woman was hissing threats at the boy, but they did nothing to intimidate the kid, though her voice was trembling from either her need to cry or just plain anger, but I had no clue which. Blowing out a breath through pursed lips, I nudged Veronica so she would let me out, pretending I didn't see the old pervert across the aisle ogling her ass when she gracefully unfolded her body like a swan rising from sleep.

She reached her arms up, stretching and twisting slightly left and right, which always did the trick. There was not one person on the plane that didn't stare openmouthed at her beauty. As far as distractions went, I couldn't ask for a better one. Sliding out of my window seat and keeping my eyes in front of me, I headed out to the lavatories separating us from the business class. Veronica's drowsy *"Oops, oh dear, I think I'm dizzy"* was drowned by the rustling of clothing when everyone jumped out to help, including the two flight attendants who were practically running to come to her aid.

My feet kept moving forward.

The red curtain wavered slightly as if someone was moving behind it just as I neared the door of the bathroom I was pretending I wanted to use. The plane dipped and we lost altitude again, but my steps didn't slow nor did my balance suffer from it. If anyone noticed, I wasn't aware of them. I kept getting closer to my goal. *You can do this. There is nothing to fear,* I reminded myself just as I reached for the curtain.

The thick fabric was yanked back before I touched it.

"You are not fine." It was the same flight attendant from earlier, her eyes narrowed on me in suspicion as she gripped the curtain in a tight-knuckled fist.

I didn't slow down.

My boots ate up the space between us, and she took a step back as if startled by my advance while she filled her lungs with air like she was about to tell me off or maybe even scream. Using my speed, I was next to her before she had time to process what was happening. I covered her mouth with one hand while pulling the curtain closed with the other. Left in the tight confines between the metal drawers behind her and me in front of her, her eyes bugged out, her nostrils flaring as she panted in fear. Lowering my face to hers, I allowed my lips to curl just enough so she could see the tips of my fangs. Her heart was hammering so hard I could feel it under my palm on her face. Such fragile creatures, humans were.

"Sleep," I whispered, taking hold of her upper arm when her eyes rolled to the back of her head.

Not a great plan, but it'd have to do. By the time she woke, she wouldn't remember what was reality and what was a dream. A perk no one but Veronica knew I had. Compelling people with your voice was a myth from human stories, and it was one that everyone laughed about.

I didn't laugh about it.

I was hiding it so I could keep my life.

Loosing precious time, I placed the woman in one of the seats in the tight place designated for the flight attendants before straightening and staring at the second curtain that would take me to the business class.

A throat cleared from somewhere in front of it and paper crinkled when the page of a book was flipped over. Behind me voices were overlapping, and among them I heard Veronica's assurances that she was okay, but they weren't very convincing, even to me. The girl was good when putting on the charm.

I slid through the curtain, my gaze darting over the top of the chairs until it stopped on the third row. He looked just like the rest of the humans, apart from two things that made him stand out: his steady heartbeat and the way his sweaty palm gripped the hand rest a tad too tight. Also, the stench of a shifter seared the inside of my nose so much my eyes watered from it. Ignoring the curious glances from those I passed, I walked up to him and crouched next to his seat, pretending I knew him by placing a hand over his forearm.

"If you make any sudden moves, I will kill you before you have a chance to blink."

Smiling sweetly, I watched his eyes widen in shock before bulging in horror when he saw my fangs. His dark, terrified gaze dropped to the pendant nestled on my throat —a symbol that made me someone's property and that was the same red color as my hair—and I watched a drop of sweat slide down the temple of his blanched face. His body trembled with the need to stand up and attack. Broad shouldered and easily over six feet, he was a male in his prime left to quake in front of a female he could break in half if given a chance. Well, any other female but me, that was.

It broadened my smile.

"You will walk with me back there." I jerked my head to the side and pointed at the extended area where I left the flight attendant. "One wrong twitch of a muscle and this plane will land with only corpses occupying it. Yours will be among them."

He lifted a shaking hand, spearing his fingers through the mass of curls sitting on top of his head. The stench of the sweat that had his shirt sticking to his body was burning my nostrils, but he blinked fast a few times before swallowing thickly and nodding his head. There was no mistaking the defeat in his eyes. Pushing up, he stood at the same time as I lifted off my crouch, my head reaching just slightly above his shoulder. My cocked eyebrow was enough for him to sigh and get moving without trying his luck. There was a good reason I was sent after him. We both knew he couldn't win.

Not with a monster like me.

The moment we were both crammed in the tight confines, I yanked the curtain closed, the sound making him flinch and face me with his knees slightly bent. Ignoring his fear, I strained to hear if Veronica was still entertaining her audience, and my own knees buckled in relief when I heard her soft chuckle.

I startled the male by taking a fistful of his shirt and yanking his face close to mine. "Can you shift here?"

"Wha-what ..." he stuttered, but I didn't have time to wait for him to get his head out of his ass.

"Can you shift?" He kept gaping at me, so I shook him to get his brain online and glared at him. "The Syndicate is sending their regards, asshole. Will you shift, or will you die here?"

"I've done nothing ..." When a muscle jumped in my jaw, he shrunk back and pressed his back to the metal drawers. "I can shift." His gravelly voice shook, the confusion in his deep brown eyes almost comical. Only, there was nothing funny about the situation for either of us.

"I will need you to shift and stay in the cargo area with the rest of the animals on board until you are transferred to the unclaimed baggage. A human will come to claim you there and take you to a safe house where you will stay as long as it takes. For the rest of your life if need be, do you understand? If you don't, we are both as good as dead." When he heard he wasn't going to die tonight, he almost dropped on his knees as his legs gave out on him. I had to hold him up by the flimsy fabric of his shirt while he nodded with gusto. "Hey." Hissing under my breath, I jerked him upright. "Look at my face and remember it as good as you remember your own. The time will come when I will need a favor. I will find you and you will do what I ask. Am I clear?"

"Of course ... anything ... please ..."

"Shift."

I had to take a step back when he instantly obeyed, and between one breath and the next a gray wolf was pinning his ears while snarling at me where the male should've been. It tucked its tail when I bared my fangs at him. Keeping him in sight from the corner of my eye, I opened the latched door to the cargo area and he bolted down like his ass was on fire. I felt like my soul was in flames from the need to go down there and join him, too. Closing it, I stiffened for what I was about to do, but they left me no choice. I would not kill a creature like me just because they told me to do it. Not if I could help it.

Sticking my head out through the curtain, I crooked my finger at the first person who turned their head to see who was coming out. A human in his sixties with unassuming features, his receding hairline making the top of his head shine in the low light of the plane took the bait.

"Come." The human got up and joined me, keeping his watery blue eyes pinned on my face. *He doesn't have that much longer to live*, I convinced myself.

Acid burned the back of my throat.

"This will not hurt," I promised him as I closed the distance between us.

My shoulders were thrown back and my head lifted high when I joined Veronica back at our seats. Sliding in, I settled into my window seat, my distant and unseeing eyes looking through the glass. She shifted slightly next to me, that small movement speaking louder than if she shouted at me.

"It's done," I told the window, not daring to look at her.

A scream from ahead of us pierced the silent air of the plane, and it was followed by one of the flight attendants yelling for a doctor. Not that anyone could save the human now. My hand fisted in my lap.

"It had to be done." Veronica sighed, sinking back in her seat in relief.

"Yes." My heart did a painful pump against my ribs once before resuming its natural slow rhythm. "Where the Syndicate is concerned … this had to be done."

Good thing she had no idea what *this* was.

For both of our sakes, I'd make sure the Council never found out exactly what I had done either.

Black Hand: Chapter Two

The sound of my footsteps as the heel of my boots clicked on the tiled floor echoed around me and bounced off the high, vaulted ceilings and walls. The marble, oak wood, and extravagant accents decorating the large mansion stood in contrast to the portraits of stern, cruel faces glaring at me from the walls. The moment anyone stepped foot through the ornate double doors into the long open foyer they were transported to some eighteenth century royal house with only one thing missing: there were no butlers or maids there. What we had was soulless killers dressed in tactical pants with their torsos bare as they stood still like statues along the walls and waited for anyone to breathe wrong. They'd strike like vipers that had been starved to death.

Maybe they were.

One might say the Syndicate loved staying in the past between the interior of the place they called home and the gladiator-type goons guarding it inside and out. With great effort, I kept my body relaxed and graceful as if I didn't have a worry in the world, the weight of my dagger on my left thigh comforting me and giving me courage not to flick my gaze to see if they were watching me. I had more worries than there were stars in the sky, but who was counting? As long as I was the only one that knew about my little *plans*, all was good.

For now.

A deep belly laugh came from the slightly opened door of the chamber, as they liked to call it. Two goons were manning it while standing with their arms folded at their backs as they stared straight ahead. The one on the right had a bad burn covering half of his face that was still in the healing process, and I couldn't help but wonder what he had done to deserve that. We didn't have to do much around here to be punished, per se. All we had to do was be at the wrong place at the wrong time. I must've been staring at his face because a deep growl rumbled in his chest and he glared at me. I jerked my gaze away from him and locked it on the slightly open door just as I stopped a foot away from them. It took everything in me not to wipe my sweaty palms on the leather of my pants.

"I'm here to report." My even, emotionless tone silenced the hum of voices coming from the other side of the damn door.

Left standing for a lot longer than necessary, I resisted the urge to turn around and leave. If I could just keep walking for days, I might go so far away that I'd never have to see any of them again. Wishful thinking, but they couldn't stop me from dreaming. Just as I stupidly was about to do that, my name was called with an invitation to enter.

I took a step.

"Brooklyn, darling. I didn't think I would see you back

so soon." The arrogant voice coming from right behind me made me falter.

"No need to mingle around when the job is done." Turning slowly to face him, my fist clenched out of my control. The goons didn't miss the move, either, but they gave me a break by raising their stares without a word. "Johnathan, I'd say it's nice to see you again but that would be a lie." My genuine smile made a line form between his perfectly styled eyebrows.

His pristine white shirt was perfectly molded to his upper body, the top two buttons open to reveal the blood-red pendant nestled there. With his hands tucked in the pockets of his black dress pants, he stood watching me with his head cocked to the side. Not too broad shouldered, Johnathan had a lean body that had fooled many to test his strength. He was thinner than most but deadly as a snake. The male would smile sweetly and honey would be pouring out of his mouth a second before he struck like a viper and ended someone's life.

He was also Veronica's lover.

"Still playing hard to get I see." Long, graceful fingers lifted to his honey blond hair, smoothing the few longer curls back while his black eyes were pinned on my face.

"Veronica didn't come with you?" Pretending he hadn't spoken, I even looked around him as if searching for her. "Let me guess, she was still doing her hair and makeup. So vain that girl. Am I right?"

"For the life of me I don't understand why she allows you to speak to her like that." Staring down his nose at me made him look uglier than he needed to be. He was a fine looking male if it wasn't for his personality. The moment he opened his mouth his good looks were flushed right down the toilet. I never understood what Veronica saw in him.

"She's my friend, and that's what friends do." Talking slowly as if he was dumb, I leaned forward as if I was about to tell him a secret. He followed suit subconsciously, which made me grin internally. "You should try getting one of those. But no one likes a kiss ass, do they?"

Johnathan's mouth twisted in anger as I spanned on my heel and pushed the door open. His hand flattened between my shoulder blades, making him look like he was good-naturedly guiding me inside. The strained smile plastered on his face was comical, but my own gloating one slipped when my eyes found three displeased stares glued to me from across a long table.

"I believe there was a good reason you kept us waiting, Brooklyn." Isaiah slanted his eyes, and the glint there told me he would kill me without batting an eye if I said a word wrong.

Jet black hair was tied in a low ponytail at the base of his head and his red lips stood out stark against his white skin. His black robes folded over his body in layers, allowing the red piping to stand out like droplets of blood being sprinkled across the fabric. It matched the attire of the other two males in the room, who were watching me with equally bloodthirsty stares. Frozen in their mid-thirties, the three Council members could've been ruling over Hollywood while being admired by men and women alike around the world. They were so perfect it almost hurt to gaze at their beauty, but that was only skin deep. They were all angelic on the outside, but there were no bigger monsters if you looked inside. Instead of admiration, they chose fear as their reason for existing. Older than dirt, all three were what supernaturals were afraid of. It was very simple in their world.

The Council of the Syndicate understood only power.

And you'd better not have more than them.

If you did, those like me were sent to fix the problem.

"Johnathan wanted to join me, Sire." Bowing my head in submission that rubbed me wrong on so many levels, I kept my voice soft and meek. "I meant no disrespect. I thought it will please you."

"What of the scum?" Frederic, sprawled on the right of Isaiah, flicked a lock of his white blonde hair over his shoulder as he trailed his fingers over the arm of the woman swaying on her feet next to him. Red rivulets flowed down her arm, thick droplets splattering the top of the table below it. His lips were stained with her blood, and I watched his tongue poke out to lick it off.

A sharp pain stabbed me at the center of my chest, and it almost doubled me over.

"Dead." The strain in my choked words couldn't be helped, and the asshole gave me a malicious grin, all fangs and teeth as if he could feel the phantom pain in my own arm throbbing.

"Excellent." Frederic purred, sinking his fangs in the woman's arm again without looking away from me. The human didn't have much longer to live.

I looked at her then. Her face was so pale it was graying on the edges of her cheeks, which stood high on a once-pretty face. Her blue eyes were unfocused and sunken on her expressionless face, and her thick hair was flattened to her skull from sweat. Her naked body was trembling and swaying while she blinked fast and tried to clear her vision. I willed her to see me, and when her gaze cleared for that one moment, I internally whispered a promise from the bottom of my soul that I would remember her face. Just like I remembered the others brought to this hell where they will die. Given as an offering for peace, or to pay off a debt, every human knew stepping in that they would not be getting out alive. It could've just been my imagination, but I thought her cracked lips lifted slightly at the corners in a sad, grateful smile before her hand went limp and she dropped in a heap on the floor. Frederic released her arm in disgust, wiping his mouth with the back of his hand.

I glared.

I couldn't help it.

"Is there a problem, dear?" The sweet tone of his voice did not match the arched eyebrow daring me to say anything that would dig my own grave.

"Not at all … Sire." I wished to remove the smirk off his face with my dagger.

But I just stood there.

"Perhaps I could talk some sense into her, Sire," the kiss-ass next to me offered casually. "It seems our Brooklyn still struggles with obedience and manners." I stiffened and my jaw clenched when he chuckled.

He still hadn't removed his hand from my back.

"Remove your hand if you'd like to keep it." Looking forward, my words were so soft that his arm dropped before I was finished talking.

"No need for that, Johnathan." My chest stopped squeezing my lungs when I heard those words. "Your father would be so proud, child." Samir, the third and last member, spoke in his calm deep voice.

My eyes darted to the portrait hanging away from all others that covered the mansion. This one was above the massive fireplace that took up almost an entire wall of the room. The same pale skin and electric green eyes stared back at me from a face resembling mine so much it couldn't be mistaken whose child I was. His black hair was the only difference between us. My red hair came from my mother, just adding to the freakshow I turned out to be among my kind.

"I do try not to soil his name and reputation, Sire." Which was true … to a point.

I didn't know much about him, only that he belonged to the Syndicate just like I did now. Or so I was told, which didn't explain why his portrait was sitting in this chamber. They told me he died in the war we had centuries ago when the rest of the supernaturals banded together in hopes to kill all of the Syndicate. My father's portrait was placed in this room to show him honor because he lost his life to protect the Council members.

I didn't believe a word of it.

According to the tales they spun, we won the war, and from that day forward even the slightest rise in power was punishable by death. They fancied themselves to be rulers and lawmakers. What the Syndicate actually depicted was the same as what the Mafia was for the humans.

Black Hand was what the rest of the supernatural world called us.

They never said it to our face.

"We should celebrate." Blinking fast, I looked away from my father's painting to see Isaiah watching me intently. "For a job well done." The smile didn't reach his eyes.

My nod was slow and wary because my mind was racing through ways I could get out of it. The three ancients were watching the internal war play out in my mind, but they grinned the moment they saw defeat in my eyes. There would be no getting out of it, though I knew any kind of celebration would be more like a massacre in this place. My deep sigh only widened their smiles.

"You are free to go, Brooklyn." Isiah twirled his hand as if shooing me off. "Do not wander too far. The party will commence in a few hours. Understood?"

"Yes, Sire." I hated the fact that they knew me too well.

"Johnathan will accompany you, yes?" Frederic was lucky I didn't jump at him and scratch his eyes out.

"I will attend alone." Jutting my chin out, I glared at him. "Or not at all."

"You must accept—" Isiah started, scowling at my glare, but Samir lifted a hand to stop the threats I could see coming.

"Alone it is, child." His caramel complexion stuck out like a sore thumb among the other two pale faces, giving him a more approachable appearance. It was just a façade, but it worked, nonetheless. "You shall sit next to me, yes?"

"Of course, Sire. It would be my honor." The words tasted like acid on my tongue.

Johnathan's face looked like he drank the acid I felt rising in my throat.

I gave Samir a genuine smile for that alone.

"Now, get out of my face," Isiah snarled baring his fangs at me, all pretense of a civilized being gone in the blink of an eye.

"As you wish, Sire." Flipping my hand with flourish, I bowed before whirling around and bolting out of the room.

Samir's guffaw echoed behind me, the sound drowning out all the cursing spilling from Isaiah's lips. I had no doubt that I'd pay for that little tantrum later. But it was so worth it to leave that kiss-ass Johnathan inside a room with a pissed-off Isiah. If I was lucky, he might have a missing eye tonight.

How was that for a celebratory gift?

My cheeks hurt from how hard I was smiling as I

hurried to find Veronica and warn her about what was coming. Because when the Syndicate was celebrating, the rest of the world mourned.

I needed to be ready for anything.

Grab your copy...
vinci-books.com/blackhand

About the Author

Maya Daniels, USA Today Bestselling and multi-award-winning supernatural suspense author, is a fun-loving woman with many talents.

She traveled the world, gaining life experiences that helped her career as an investigative journalist, as well as her storytelling. Maya writes compelling tales of magic, mythical creatures, loyalty, and life-changing friendships with snarky female characters—much like herself.

Her travels have taken her to Europe, Africa, Asia, Australia, and America. Born with her feet in motion, she currently resides in Ohio, spinning her next epic story that you will not want to put down.

Her biggest 'sins' are her love of chocolate and coffee—through an IV drip! One to never sit still, Maya practices Reiki healing, different types of martial arts, reads about the arcane, talks to furry creatures more than humans, picks up a sledgehammer for home improvement, and travels with her fated mate, seeking her own adventures.